Thailand with the Tycoon

Alexia Adams

Copyright

Thailand with the Tycoon

By Alexia Adams
Copyright 2019 by Alexia Adams

Published by:
Alexia Adams
Suite 377
255 Newport Drive
Port Moody, BC V3H 5H1
Canada

Contact: Alexia@alexia-adams.com
www.alexia-adams.com

Edited by Brenda Chin and Amanda Bidnall, PhD

Ebook ISBN 978-0-9939126-8-9
Print ISBN 978-1-9991756-5-8

First Ebook Edition March 2019
First Print Edition September 2020
Product of Canada

Chapter One

Caleb ran his fingers along the rock face, searching for a hold. He dislodged a pebble and it bounced down the cliff until he couldn't hear it anymore. That meant he was near the top … and a fall now would definitely kill him. God, he was exhausted. Why the hell had he started his ascent this late in the day? If he wasn't off the mountain soon, he'd either have to risk the climb in the dark or cling where he was until dawn.

But after the week he'd had, the need to escape the office and breathe fresh, clean, non-profit-oriented air had led him to his current situation. Starting his own venture capital firm—getting in at the start of some amazing businesses and ideas—had sounded like fun. But it had quickly morphed into constant meetings and investment reports. At least falling 700 meters down the Stawamus Chief would be a better death than his father's: having a heart attack Friday night and being found Monday morning on the boardroom floor. No one had missed him for an entire weekend, because he'd practically lived at the office.

But Caleb wasn't ready to die just yet. There were a lot of things—a lot of women—he still wanted to do.

His fingers found a good hold, and he hauled his sorry

ass another few centimeters closer to the summit. An eagle soared overhead as if mocking his puny efforts. Dangling on a granite dome was a damn sight more invigorating than reading about the next great investment, but it wasn't how he wanted to spend his night. He pushed through his tiredness and concentrated on one hold after another until he crested the top, too exhausted to celebrate. Lying on his back, he waited for his heart rate to return to normal while the coldness of the stone seeped into his burning muscles. He rolled to his side and stared at the blue-green water of Howe Sound. He'd lived on the west coast of Canada all his life and traveled around the globe more times than he could count, but this sight always took his breath away. The pristine coastal mountains in the background hinted at adventure. And freedom.

Something kicked at his foot and Caleb turned warily, hoping it wasn't a black bear trying to determine if he was edible. But unless the local wildlife had invaded an Italian shoe store, it was a human standing over him. And considering the inappropriate shoes, expensive suit, and silk tie still tightly fastened at the neck, it could only be one person: Harrison Mackenzie.

"Come to make sure I survived?" Caleb asked, pushing himself into a sitting position.

"When I didn't see your broken body at the base of the Chief, I assumed you'd made it," Harrison said, his voice as always carefully neutral. You never knew if he was excited or depressed. It made him a fabulous lawyer but an annoying friend.

"Great to know you were worried. What's up?"

Harrison and nature did not go together, as evidenced by his attire.

Harrison's hands clenched tightly at his sides, providing the only sign something was wrong.

"You need to come back to Vancouver. I've had them reopen the Sea to Sky gondola. The helicopter is waiting in the parking lot." Harrison turned as though expecting Caleb to obediently follow.

"Why?" Caleb stayed where he was, partly because his muscles weren't ready to comply with his brain's demand to move, but mostly because he hated being told what to do. That's why he'd left the family business to his brother and branched out on his own. Unfortunately, he then became wildly successful, creating his own leg-hold trap of board meetings, contract negotiations, and endless investment reports. He should have opened a rock-climbing school or one of those ninja warrior gyms. Maybe that would be his next challenge: to finally do something he was passionate about. Perhaps it would soothe the itch inside that pushed him to take ever-greater risks.

"I'll tell you on the way." Harrison's leather-soled shoes slipped on the smooth granite, and instinctively Caleb leapt to his feet to stop his friend from falling. Great lawyers were replaceable, but ones who put up with Caleb's shit and took his calls at three in the morning were a little rarer.

"We need to hurry," Harrison said, once he'd regained his footing.

Caleb crossed his arms, ignoring the protest of his muscles. "Unless you tell me why it's so urgent I go back to Vancouver, I'm heading to Whistler for the weekend." He narrowed his eyes. "If this is my mother's latest way to summon me, you'd better start looking for a new job on Monday."

He had a vague recollection of his admin assistant reminding him that his mother was back in town and expected him to pay her a visit. But he'd spent enough years dancing attendance on that woman. He was done playing her games. Besides, her lame attempts at pretending she cared were always simply a prelude to a request for money. She'd already gone through what his father had left to her. And with his brother's company failing, she'd turned to Caleb to maintain her lavish lifestyle. In short, she expected him to pay her damn bills, even though she hadn't called him once on his birthday since he'd left home at eighteen.

Harrison kept walking, not even turning around to answer. "I know better than to get between you and your mother. It's Ian. Your brother has had a heart attack. And he won't settle until he speaks with you."

"Shit." Ian was only eight years older than Caleb. Forty was way too early to have heart problems. At least Patrick, their dad, had made it to fifty before he fell apart.

Caleb followed Harrison down the path toward the gondola. Far below, he could see a helicopter in the overflow parking lot that wasn't used this late in the season.

"Is Ian going to be okay?" There were enough years between them that they'd never been close as brothers. Ian had insisted that Caleb was making a huge mistake when he left the family hotel business to start his own ventures. His doubts had been a massive incentive for Caleb to prove his brother wrong by out-earning him.

Once that had been accomplished, the tension between them had notched up another degree. Now, they only saw each other three times a year: at Mother's birthday party, the Doyle Destinations AGM—Caleb still held a minority share—and at the major fundraiser for the charity their mother had set up in memory of Patrick Doyle. Not that Claire wanted to memorialize a man who had been a shadow in all their lives. She simply liked being the center of attention, and this was her way to get it.

"They were still running tests when I left," Harrison replied as they got in the gondola for the quick ride down the mountain. "His secretary found him slumped over his desk and called 911."

"Who called you?"

"Your sister-in-law. Evidently, as soon as Ian regained consciousness, he started asking for you and became agitated. When you didn't answer your phone, Sarah called me and requested I hunt you down."

"My phone is locked in my car," Caleb said. The gondola doors opened, and a cool breeze off the ocean swept over them. The warmth and adrenaline from his climb had worn off, leaving him chilled. He was going to hurt like a bitch tomorrow.

Harrison shouted as the helicopter blades started to turn. "I'll drive your car back and leave the keys in your condo."

Caleb handed over his car keys and ran for the open

helicopter door. He'd barely got his seatbelt buckled before it lifted off for the flight back to the city.

***

The rubber soles of his rock-climbing shoes squeaked on the polished tile floor of St. Paul's Hospital. The sterile air was a sharp contrast to the pure mountain freshness he'd been breathing half an hour ago.

The woman at the information desk did a double-take when she glanced up from her computer. "The emergency department is down that hall," she said, pointing to her left.

He quirked an eyebrow at her reply then followed her gaze down his body. He hadn't taken the time to change out of his skin-tight climbing gear, and his arms and legs were covered with the myriad scratches he'd gotten rubbing intimately against Mother Nature. He looked like he'd been dragged behind a bus for half a block.

"I'm fine. I'm here to see my brother, Ian Doyle. Has he been transferred to a ward yet? I was told he had a heart attack earlier today."

"Oh, sorry." Her eyes made one more appreciative pass over his body before returning to her computer. "Ian Doyle is in the cardiac unit, room 710." She gave him directions to the ward then flashed another smile. "I'll be here until eight if there's anything else I can help with." Her gaze locked on his. "Anything at all."

He gave her a smile and a wink to make her day before striding down the hall. If there was one thing he'd learned, it was that nice, normal girls spelled trouble.

Like, "wanting a relationship" trouble. It was far better to stick to shallow women who were only interested in a good time. Because that was all he had to offer.

He paused outside the designated room, getting his game face ready. His brother's agitated voice, as well as his sister-in-law's calming one, floated through the thin walls.

"Hey, who said you could take a holiday?" Caleb said in the cheeriest tone he could manage. He wrapped an arm around his sister-in-law, Sarah, to give her some support. His mother sat in a chair the other side of the bed, doing something on her phone. She didn't even glance up at the arrival of her youngest child.

"Caleb." Ian's pale face relaxed a fraction, and the heart monitor showed a decrease in his pulse rate. "You have to go to Thailand for me."

That wasn't the request he'd expected. Caleb turned questioning eyes on the petite woman next to him. His twin five-year-old niece and nephew were absent, probably with one of Sarah's family. They were far too young to be without a dad. Caleb would do anything for them.

"Ian was supposed to leave for Thailand tomorrow to finalize negotiations for a new hotel," his sister-in-law said, her voice quavering. There was a desperate fear in her brown eyes. "But as you can see, he can't go."

Caleb took in the beeping monitors that counted his brother's heartbeat, blood pressure, oxygen levels, and other functions the healthy took for granted.

He tightened his arm around Sarah. He'd always liked her; she was the opposite of his mother. Her quiet strength and no-nonsense approach suited Ian completely. How his brother had convinced such a lovely woman to join their frigid family, he had no idea.

"Surely that can wait until you're better," Caleb replied. It was no secret that the hotel business his father had started in the early eighties was facing extinction. People expected something different from their travel experience now, and Doyle Destinations hadn't kept up with the times. It wasn't Ian's fault that their father had so meticulously groomed his eldest son to follow his lead that he'd forgotten how to think independently.

"No, it has to be now. There's another bidder. We have to buy it within the next week. This is the best chance I've got to turn the company around. Without this resort, we'll go bankrupt in eighteen months." Ian's heart rate accelerated while he talked, and his face turned even whiter.

"Please, Caleb." Sarah's soft plea stabbed him right in his ice-shrouded heart and did more to convince him than his brother's recitation. Damsels in distress were his weakness. He could never resist playing the hero. But one more property wasn't going to turn Ian's company around. The whole enterprise needed a major overhaul.

He turned back to his brother. "All right. I'll go. But you promise to get better and be out of here by the time I get back." He gripped Ian's hand where it fidgeted on the bedsheet and gave it a slight squeeze. The differences in their ages and temperaments meant they'd never been close. And given the arctic vortex they'd grown up in, a hand squeeze was about all either of them was comfortable with.

The icy wind that was their mother chose that moment to look up from her phone. In Claire Doyle's mind, the world revolved around her.

"Before you leave, Caleb dear, I need to have word with you about my finances." Trust his mother to discuss money at his brother's hospital bedside. A smile from her would have shocked Caleb into his own heart attack. There were a lot of things you could change in life; Mother wasn't one of them.

"Talk to my accountant," he replied. "I need to go pack."

It really wasn't the time to go gallivanting off to the other side of the globe, but at least this trip to Thailand would warm him up after the chill of being in the same room as his mother. A few quiet days of pampering in a luxury Thai resort while he negotiated on his brother's behalf would be his reward for having to run two companies until Ian was back on his feet again.

And here he'd thought falling down a 700-meter cliff was all he'd have to worry about today.

***

Malee dug her fingernails into the dashboard of her cousin's open-top Jeep. So far, the day had been a complete disaster. This was her first job in three months, and she was on the verge of losing it before she'd even started. The early bus she'd intended to take into the city had been full. Then she'd had to beg her cousin Bodin, her least favorite relative but the only one with a vehicle, to drive her to Nan. Instead of being cooled by the bus's air conditioner, she was being buffeted with hot, humid air. Monsoon season was never pleasant. Coupled with inner turmoil and a dash of sheer panic, Malee was on the verge of a meltdown. Possibly literally.

To top off her day from hell, the pharmacy where they'd stopped to collect her grandmother's prescription had been out of the antibiotic. Phoning around to find the drug had eaten up another precious hour.

She should have let Bodin collect the medicine after he dropped her off at the airport, but he'd been so distracted that she had to remind him three times on the drive from their remote village to stop at the drugstore. He'd always played the village idiot, but he seemed to have ascended to the king of fools' throne recently. Still, he was a close relation. And you had to respect relatives, no matter their IQ. Family was the center around which life revolved.

And the nucleus of Malee's life was her maternal grandparents. *Yai*, her grandmother, had been battling pneumonia for three months now, and if she didn't complete this course of antibiotics, she could end up back in hospital, or worse. A tremor swept through Malee, and she clutched the dash tighter.

Bodin took another corner too fast, and she clenched her eyes shut to avoid seeing the inevitable collision. The memory of another car crash flitted through her mind. What she wouldn't give to forget…

"Malee, about this job… Don't screw it up." Bodin took his eyes off the road to stare at her and narrowly missed a minivan with a flat tire at the side of the road. At least her horrified gasp at the near-miss gave her time to formulate an appropriate reply. He'd already inferred six times in the past two hours that she couldn't cope with a simple translation assignment. *I'm not the stupid one here, Bodin.*

"I am qualified, cousin." She put as much deference into her tone as possible. Thai custom dictated that she be respectful of her older relative, even if he was being a condescending jerk. Since her grandfather's accident, Bodin had become the de facto head of the family, a position that commanded deference even if the incumbent didn't.

But thirteen years in the Western world had dulled that instinct in Malee. She forced a smile. "If there's one thing I can do, it's speak both Thai and English fluently." She'd lived in London with her mother from the age of twelve.

It was a simple enough assignment. She was to collect Ian Doyle and translate for him in his negotiations to buy the run-down resort near where her grandparents lived in northeastern Thailand. The original owners had never made a success of the place, so she had no idea why this Canadian figured he could do better. Most tourists to Thailand expected pretty beaches and wild nightlife, not dense jungle, masses of mosquitoes, and minimal electricity after dark.

The only visitors to this part of the country were backpackers seeking the "real" Thailand. Like the country had to stay in the seventeenth century to be authentic.

Well, you didn't get much more "real" than unemployed. And if she didn't arrive at the airport in ten minutes, that would remain her reality.

It was more than just her job on the line. If this Canadian hotelier bought the resort and fixed it up, it would provide much-needed work for the little village where most of her relatives still lived. Maybe Malee's mother could come home from London at last. The whole family could be together after fifteen years apart. A flicker of hope overrode the terror of her cousin's driving for an all-too-brief second.

"You sure you don't want me to wait? I can drive you both back to Pakang Yao," Bodin said as he screeched to a halt in front of the arrivals terminal at Nan Nakhon Airport.

Letting her reckless cousin drive her new boss would undoubtedly result in instant dismissal. "It's okay. I'm told he has his transport organized."

Bodin cut the engine and put his hand on her arm, stopping her from getting out. "Malee, about the resort. You know it would mean a lot to the village if it was reopened. You have to convince this foreigner to buy it."

"I'm just assigned to translate."

"You can do more than that. A pretty girl like you, I'm sure you can be persuasive if you want."

Bodin, you are an arse. First you doubt I can speak English well enough, and now you want me to flirt to get a farang *to buy a pile of junk that no reasonable Thai person would take two looks at?*

She lowered her head so he couldn't read the anger blazing in her eyes and cheeks. "The info I received from the translation agency said he's married with two children."

Bodin frowned and kept hold of her. "I'm not asking you to disgrace the family. Just show him the potential of the place. Come on, cousin. Do it for the villagers. Think of all the jobs you'll bring back so the young people don't leave for the city."

Like she needed more stress to add to her already churning stomach. Bodin wasn't the first to bring it up. Word had already spread about the potential sale. The village's fate rested on her shoulders. "I'll try. But I'm not sure how much I can do." She climbed out of the vehicle before her cousin could launch into a lecture.

"Make it happen, Malee." With those parting words, he restarted the Jeep, slammed it back into first gear, and sped off to the blaring of horns from the cars he cut off.

Malee tucked her bag with her change of clothes under her arm and strode toward the airport doors. Bodin's vehicle was never clean, and she hadn't wanted to dirty her dress before she arrived. *Please, let one thing go right today and give me enough time to change.* Mr. Doyle was coming by private jet, and she'd only been given an approximate time of arrival.

The automatic doors opened as she approached, and a very tall, blond man strode out, looking like he'd come to claim Thailand for his own. Everything about the man shrieked conqueror. His pale hair glinted in the sunshine, showing hints of red. A strong jaw and full lips next grabbed her attention. His eyes were hidden behind mirrored aviator sunglasses, but based on his coloring, they were probably either blue or green.

A good Thai woman would lower her gaze and shuffle past without ogling. Malee wasn't a typical Thai woman. She wanted to examine every inch of him. The cultural war within her was damned difficult.

About to move around him as he stood staring at the passing traffic, she stopped abruptly. He wasn't dressed in shorts and sandals. Not even a T-shirt. Instead he wore a full suit and tie that emphasized his broad chest and lean physique. It couldn't be…

"Mr. Doyle?" she asked, praying she was mistaken. This hunk of manhood would make even a proper Thai woman forget about appropriate conduct. A quick glance at his left hand, clutching a briefcase, showed no sign of a wedding band. Was he one of *those* men who took it off when he traveled? The thought alone was enough to turn her stomach. "Sorry, I must be mistaken."

"I'm Doyle," he said. Damn if his voice wasn't dark molten chocolate. "You're not by chance Ms. Wattana?" He removed his sunglasses as his gaze slid over her. The interest in his green eyes was quickly replaced by cool detachment. Had she imagined it? Unfortunately, it didn't stop a shiver of awareness from sweeping through her.

She didn't dare glance at the reflective glass of the airport building to see what she looked like. She could only imagine that her hair was tangled around her head in great clumps, since she'd been holding onto the dashboard too desperately to secure it. She could taste the dust on her lips, feel a trickle of perspiration pool in her bra. This was not the picture of professionalism she'd intended to present. And here he was, having come off an international flight, looking immaculate and sexier than any married man had a right to be.

She put her palms together and bent forward in the customary Thai greeting. "*Sawatdee-kah.* Yes, I'm Malee. I apologize for my clothing. I'd intended to change before you arrived." Her shorts were a couple of years old and faded in the backside, her T-shirt declared Westlife as the best boy band ever, and her sandals had seen better days as well. She'd planned to throw the whole lot in the rubbish after she'd changed.

Mr. Doyle's eyes swept over her again, leaving a trail of tingles in their wake. He gestured at his own outfit. "You're dressed more appropriately than me. It must be forty degrees Celsius. I'm going to melt if I stay in this suit much longer."

"It will be cooler once we get into the mountains. The information package I received said you already had transportation arranged to the resort location." She forced her eyes from the column of tanned skin that appeared as he loosened his tie and undid the top three buttons of his shirt.

Puzzlement flicked in his gaze. "Do I? I skipped over all the technicalities about how to get there as I concentrated on the hotel specifications." He pulled out his phone and began searching.

Malee tilted her head. From the details she'd been provided, Ian Doyle had been in discussions about the property for several months now. Her job was simply to translate as required and ensure there were no items being discussed that he didn't understand.

"There it is. I'm to be met by you here and then we are to proceed to the car rental desk, where a vehicle has been reserved. Do you drive, Malee?"

He turned those amazing green eyes on her once more. "Yes, I drive, but not very well." Certainly not on mountain roads ruled by huge buses and transport trucks and littered with pedestrians, farm animals, wildlife, and hitchhiking tourists willing to risk their lives to save a few baht. And definitely not with this definition of distraction sitting next to her.

"That's fine. I can drive if you can navigate." He reentered the terminal building, and Malee followed behind. Maybe she should call Bodin and get him to drive them to the resort. But subjecting Mr. Doyle to her cousin's death-defying driving style seemed a bit extreme.

At the rental desk, he smiled at the woman behind the counter. A flush crept up the attendant's face and her eyes took on a dazed quality. God, was Malee wearing the same stupid expression? The rental car woman shot a look at Malee and seemed to dismiss her as competition. "How can I help you, sir?"

"You have a car reserved in my brother's name. Ian Doyle. I—"

"Your brother?" Malee blurted out. "So you're not married?"

Chapter Two

Bloody hell. She had not just said that out loud, had she? But the flare in Mr. Doyle's eyes told her she had. And he hadn't misunderstood her outburst. Weren't translators supposed to carefully consider their words to convey the most accurate interpretation? She cleared her throat and tried to inflect just the right amount of curiosity into her question. "I mean, you're not *Ian* Doyle?"

"No, I'm Caleb. Ian's younger—and unmarried—brother. No girlfriend either, if that makes a difference."

Difference? It made him downright dangerous.

"I'm sorry. I was told to meet Ian Doyle. Are you taking his place?" Now she was veering into stupid territory. What was it about the man that scrambled her brain?

"Yes. My brother wasn't able to travel. Unfortunately, I'm not fully up to speed on the resort he's interested in purchasing, so any information you can provide will be invaluable."

She nodded. The place was a disaster. She had a hard time believing anyone would attempt to resurrect what had been a failure before it even began.

"I understand your negotiations to purchase the property are to occur tomorrow. That doesn't give you a lot of time to check the place out." But even a cursory glance would show him the hotel needed a lot of work. Bodin was insane if she thought a little persuasion on her part would make a difference.

"I've moved the meeting to next Monday. I want to fully investigate this potential purchase. I asked Ian's secretary to contact your agency and request your services for the full week. Did they not call you?"

"I hadn't heard. But I can assure you that it's fine." Except he was likely to take one look at the place and jump back on his private jet to Canada.

"Perfect." His smile revealed a dimple in his right cheek, and she quickly looked away. A whole week in this man's company might just reduce her to a drooling fool, but it would be worth every second. For the money the job would bring in, of course.

Her racing pulse called her a liar. Men like Caleb Doyle didn't come into her life too often—or ever. She might be dedicated to her family and integrating back into Thai society, but that didn't mean she couldn't enjoy a little eye candy. Her Western upbringing had taken over again.

The woman at the rental desk spoke perfect English, so there was no need for Malee to translate. Instead, she scrolled through her phone, pretending to search for the message from her agency. If she didn't get a grip soon, she'd make a complete idiot of herself. And prove her cousin correct.

A message from her mother popped into her inbox,

asking how the job hunting was going. Mum was stuck in London. Her job there was too well-paid to give up. Since she was the only one receiving a regular salary, she'd have to stay until Malee found something that could support her grandparents, her mum, and herself. Malee replied that she had a job for a week and a lead on a longer one, and she made a mental note to write a proper letter tonight. There was no internet in her village. It was like living in the 1980s, but without Madonna pretending to be a virgin. No wonder all the young people left.

She didn't need to look up to know when Mr. Doyle turned his attention back to her. A tingle trickled down her spine. "We're all set. How far is it to the resort?"

"About three hours, depending on the traffic. If you need to send any messages, you should do so now. Cellular service is sporadic outside of Nan."

"I'm good. I texted my office that I'd arrived when the plane touched down. I try to avoid my phone as much as possible."

"Then you're going to love your new resort." She put as much enthusiasm as she could into the pronouncement, and a glimmer touched his eyes.

"Why do I get the feeling that's a warning?"

She hid her unease behind a fake smile. "I'm just here to translate. I'll leave the decision making to you."

A wall of hot, humid air hit them as they exited the terminal and made their way to the rental vehicle. Malee was pleased to see it was a newer-model SUV, complete with airbags and all the regular safety features her cousin's Jeep lacked.

As Caleb put his suitcase in the back, he asked, "Where's your bag? I assumed you'd be staying at the resort as well. I read it's quite a trek to the nearest village."

She froze, her hand on the passenger's-side door handle. "You're staying at Primarayatha Resort? The one in the mountains near Pakang Yao village?" She'd figured he'd arranged to stay in one of the few luxury houses dotted around the countryside. The place he was here to investigate was only fit to accommodate mold spores and spiders.

"Yes, of course. What better way to determine if it's a good fit for my brother's hotel portfolio than to experience its ambiance and service for myself?"

Damn. She couldn't mislead the man into a three-hour drive to sleep in a ruin. By the time they got there, it would be too late to make the trek back to Nan safely. Her cousin's plea rang in her head, but she had to listen to her conscience.

She lowered her eyes to the ground. "Mr. Doyle—"

"Call me Caleb. And please look at me when you speak. I can't have a conversation with the top of your head."

She raised her gaze and was caught for a moment in the intensity of his. What was she about to say? Oh, right. That her one-week assignment was about to shrink to five minutes. "Caleb…" His name was delicious on her tongue. She hauled in a deep breath to steady her voice. "It seems you've been misinformed about the state of the resort. It's been deserted for several years and needs a lot of work."

He lowered his sunglasses, spearing her with his green eyes. "Really?"

"Yes."

He replaced his aviators and ran a hand through his blond hair before shrugging. "I've come this far. I might as well see the place. And I've spent the night clinging to the side of a mountain with only a rope keeping me from certain death. I'm sure a stay in a broken-down hotel won't kill me."

She admired his determination if not his self-preservation skills. "All right. If you're sure."

Fortunately, she had a cellular signal long enough to navigate them out of the city and onto the highway toward her grandparents' village and the resort. Maybe it wasn't in such bad shape. She hadn't been there since it closed. Perhaps someone had taken an interest in it and cleaned up? If they were trying to attract buyers, it made sense. Although she was sure she would have heard something about that in the village. Maybe Bodin had, and that's why he was sure Mr. Doyle would be persuadable. Still, an uneasy niggling in her stomach kept her on edge.

And when she was nervous, she talked. Incessantly. To start, she pointed out local landmarks that she remembered, making a few things up when she couldn't think of something to say. Once they were out of town, she waxed lyrical about the vegetation and animals they spotted. Her dissertation on water buffalos was a low-light that she was sure to relive in her darkest moments. Poor Caleb. He undoubtedly thought he'd been saddled with a lunatic. He was probably eagerly anticipating some solitude in a decrepit hotel after this car journey.

"How long have you been in the hotel industry?" she asked when, finally, her knowledge of Northern Thailand's flora and fauna ran dry.

An amused smile played on his lips as he glanced briefly at her. "Doyle Destinations has been around since the '80s. My father started the company, and my older brother has continued in his place since my dad's passing."

"I'm sorry to hear about your father. Mine is gone as well."

"Condolences."

She shrugged. "It's been many years. Sometimes I find it hard to remember his face." She shifted uncomfortably, recalling her father's death, then shoved the memory away. Right now, as they drove the same route that had witnessed the end of her parents' marriage, was not the time to dwell on that. At least Caleb was a much better driver than her cousin or father. Even though it was his first time on these roads—and based on his talk about sleeping on the side of a mountain, he had a wild side—she felt safe with him. His strong hands held the steering wheel lightly, and there were scratches on the back of his hand and along his arms where he'd rolled up the sleeves of his shirt. Was he a fighter? Or did he have an uncontrollable cat?

There was a small scar along his jaw and another along his hairline near his temple, but the rest of him was close to perfection. He was gorgeous, successful, with an undeniable air of power tinged with a hint of mischief. He had to be a real player not to have been snared by some woman before now.

A sigh escaped her lips, and he turned to look at her.

"Everything okay? If you direct me to the resort, I'll drive you home afterward. I don't expect you to stay with me if it's been abandoned."

"Thank you." It was better for him to think she was worried about staying at a bad hotel than wondering why he was still single. Maybe he was away so frequently that he rarely had time to date. "Do you travel often, visiting potential resorts?"

"I travel, but not with the hotel business. My brother runs it. I have my own company."

"You don't work for the family enterprise?"

"No. I don't like being told what to do." A rueful smile lifted his lips. "I'm very stubborn."

He'd need to be if he intended to stay at the resort by himself. It wasn't for the faint of heart.

Fortunately, traffic was light, and they arrived at her grandparent's village before she could entertain him with details of her own failings. Caleb slowed as the road became congested with pedestrians, mopeds, carts, dogs, the occasional chicken, and children darting between them all.

She glanced at her watch and bit her bottom lip. *Just ask him. He's easygoing.* After all, he'd asked her to call him by his first name. And look him in the eye. He wasn't some stuck-up *farang.* Bloody hell, he'd listened to her prattle on for nearly two hours without so much as a groan. She wanted to groan herself. It'd be easier to ignore his good looks if he was arrogant, or an idiot like Bodin. *Surely, he wouldn't mind a little detour.*

"Would it be okay if we stopped for two minutes so I can drop off my grandmother's prescription? She's supposed to take her next pill at five o'clock, and I'm not sure I'll be back by then."

He nodded. "Just give me directions." As he slowly negotiated the congested street, his eyes eating up the chaos, he asked, "Have your grandparents lived here their whole lives?"

"Since they married. My gran is from one of the local hill tribes, she's Mien. And she's more than a bit eccentric, which she plays off as being part of her culture. But it's not—it's just her. I spent a summer with her people, and they're all normal.

"My grandfather is from Vietnam," she continued. "He moved here at the start of the war. He said he couldn't kill anyone, no matter their politics or which language they spoke. My grandparents are usually pretty active people, but my *pu...*" She shook her head, realizing she'd slipped back into Thai. "My grandfather broke his leg a few months ago, riding his motorbike up a steep hill while chasing a stray goat, and my grandmother has been battling a lung infection. I moved back here to help them out until they're both able to get around unaided." And to escape the pitying glances from her mother and coworkers following the demise of her latest pathetic relationship. But Caleb definitely didn't need to know that tidbit.

As it was, he probably regretted asking her the question. But instead of giving her an exasperated look, his smile deepened. He was either genuinely nice or very good at faking it.

The village was small, and within a few minutes, he'd pulled up in front of her grandparents' house. The cement block building was clean, thanks to her grandmother's fastidiousness. Caleb hadn't even switched the engine off before all the neighborhood children surrounded the vehicle, eager to see who had arrived.

"You bringing a man to meet your yai and pu? He going to marry you? *Wao*, nice car. How much he pay? He got good job? He going to take you away?" The children's excited chatter greeted her as she stepped out of the vehicle. *Brilliant, Malee. Teach the local children English so they can embarrass you the first time you bring a guest to the village.*

Expecting Caleb to remain in the SUV, she was surprised when he got out. But then, he'd flown from Canada and driven for two hours. He was probably desperate for a stretch.

Sure enough, he raised his hands to the sky and swung his torso around in a circle. Malee stood and stared at the way his shirt clung to the muscles of his body as he moved. *Damn.*

His eyes were laughing when they caught her gaze. "Your grandparents?"

No need for a mirror to know her face had heated at being caught ogling. "Um, would you like to come in?"

"Sure. But I do want to get to the resort tonight…"

"Yes. I'll be quick."

She swung open the door, hurried into the room, and turned toward the sofa, where her grandfather had spent much of the last three-and-a-half months. He was there, but so was her grandmother. Sitting astride him. Both of them naked.

Malee swiveled around and ran straight into Caleb. He wrapped one arm around her waist, took the paper bag from her hand, placed it silently on the table, and stepped backward out of the house. He closed the door behind them before their interruption was even noticed by her grandparents.

"Oh, God. I'm sorry you had to see that," she said as they stood on the front step, her face on fire. She was sorry *she'd* seen it. Someone really needed to invent that memory-wipe device from the *Men in Black* movies.

Caleb's arm lingered around her waist, and it was a long breath before he dropped it. Even after he moved his hand, the sensation lingered on her skin. "I didn't need to see it, but your grandparents have restored my faith that passionate marriages can last."

She stared up into his gorgeous green eyes awash with laughter. "Not a lot of happy marriages in your family?"

The laughter faded, and he strode back toward the car. "No."

"I'm sorry, I shouldn't have asked you something so personal."

"Don't worry about it." He snapped his seatbelt on and glanced at her bare legs. Her pulse quickened, and an unfamiliar tingle ran down the back of her thighs.

For the first time in her life, she wished she was the type of woman to indulge in a brief affair. Caleb Doyle could never be more than Mr. Right Now. She wanted a safe, steady man in her life. Not one who slept on mountainsides or willingly stayed in derelict buildings.

She held back another sigh. This job had potential disaster written all over it.

***

Caleb gripped the wheel tighter as the tires slipped on the loose gravel. Deep ruts in the road, caused by rivers of water rushing down the mountainside, had made driving treacherous. As the lane straightened for a nanosecond, he glanced over at his companion. Malee clutched the armrest so tightly that his damage deposit would be used to buff the nail prints out of the leather.

She had to be really terrified to stop talking. He'd enjoyed her quirky travelogue as they'd passed through various villages and towns. And he was pretty sure he'd ace any exam on the life and mating habits of water buffalo. He could have listened to her plummy British accent all day, every word sprinkled with warmth and humor and love for her country. If he wasn't careful, it could become an issue. He was already physically attracted to her. Liking her as well spelled trouble—all in capital letters.

When she'd first spoken to him at the airport, his blood had all headed south. He could imagine his name dropping huskily from her full lips, her tanned skin flushed with pleasure, amber-flecked chocolate eyes begging him for more. Her long, dark hair would cling to her glistening back, her full breasts bouncing before him as he brought her to the pinnacle of pleasure before tumbling over himself.

What the hell was wrong with him? Since when did he lust over an employee? He couldn't touch her. Shouldn't touch her. She worked for him, however temporarily.

Her beauty, though, was undeniable. Exotic. Intriguing. The way she moved was unconsciously sensuous, and her face, when they'd walked in on her grandparents, had been priceless. She'd been three parts embarrassed, one part amazed, and one part proud. He'd like to think that in his later years, he'd still be having some afternoon delight with his favorite lady.

But more than just outwardly beautiful, she appeared beautiful on the inside as well. Her whole face lit with love when she spoke of her grandparents. And she'd put her own life on hold to help them out. Could she really be that nice? Then he remembered her warning back at the airport. She'd seemed truly concerned about him staying at the rundown hotel. He stole another quick glance at her profile and was not pleased at the way his mouth automatically curved into a smile.

The undercarriage of the vehicle bottomed out on a huge rut and brought his attention back to the so-called road. "How much farther?" he asked.

"Another five minutes or so. I don't think anyone has been up this way in ages."

"No." His throat tightened. How could Ian have pinned his hopes for restoring the company's fortunes on this resort? Was his brother delusional, or just incompetent?

Another stab of guilt sliced through his gut. If Caleb hadn't been so determined to get out of his brother's shadow and set out on his own, to prove himself, he would have known how bad the company's financial situation had become. He could have stepped in sooner. But when he worked with Ian, every suggestion he made was met with, "That's not how Dad would have wanted it done." It had made his blood boil.

"You speak English with a British accent," he said to take his mind off this fool's mission he was on. He should have turned around at the airport when Malee had mentioned the derelict state of the resort. But he'd already come this far, and it would be petty to tell his brother he'd rejected the property without even seeing it. The lure of spending more time with his beautiful translator had also factored into his decision to stay.

"I moved to England to be with my mother when I was twelve and only recently returned to Thailand when my grandparents needed a little help." Her laugh held more embarrassment than amusement. "Obviously my living with them has put a damper on their marital bliss."

He chuckled and dared another glance at her. A blush stained her cheeks, and she bit her bottom lip. Did she realize how seductive she was? With no thought to the reality of the situation, his groin flooded with heat.

He forced his mind to business rather than pleasure. "Are there any other hotels or resorts around here?"

"Not within an hour's drive. There are a few treks that come into the area, but they're mostly backpacker types who like to stay with the hill tribe people. There's nothing super special here to draw tourists." She pressed her lips together tightly, as though she hadn't meant to say the last part.

"I don't know about that." He pretended to check out the view through her window. "Sometimes it takes an outsider to see things that locals assume no one else is interested in." His eyes were drawn back to her again, but she stared out the window. Was she trying to see what he did?

They rounded one more bend and the road veered inland, away from the side of the mountain. The vegetation was shorter here, having been pruned at some point in the past. Eventually, the resort came into view. His gut clenched tighter than a newbie climber's grip on the safety line.

Malee hadn't been lying about the state of the place. The whole ground floor of the building was overrun by vegetation. Vines dangled from some of the upper balconies, and the few remaining spots of white on the gray cement looked more like blemishes than the original paint covering.

At least the windows he could see still had their glass, and the roof seemed intact. Caleb had some hope that the inside would prove more welcoming than the outside. At the moment, the place was good only as a location for a horror film—the kind where desperate travelers seek shelter in an old hotel and spend a night of terror, only one making it out alive. He paused, waiting for the eerie music to begin.

He stopped the SUV in what was once a parking lot. Pulling in a moisture-laden lungful of air, he stretched his back. At least it was slightly cooler here than in Nan.

Malee came to stand beside him as he leaned against the vehicle. "She's got good bones," she said softly, as though to appease any malevolent spirits in the area.

As he swung his gaze to his companion, he caught sight of the vista, and for the first time he could understand why someone would build here in the first place. A lush, green landscape of mountains and valleys lay before him. He could probably see all the way to the Laos border. It was a bucolic scene marred only by the ominous black clouds approaching rapidly.

"And a great view," he added. "I'm just going to check that I can get inside, and then I'll take you back your grandparents' house." He didn't like the look of the approaching storm and hoped he could make it down to the valley and back again before it struck. Maybe he should spend the night in the village. He hadn't seen any visitor accommodation, however. And he wasn't sure he'd be comfortable spending the night on Malee's sofa, considering what her grandparents been doing on it an hour ago.

The front door of the hotel was secured, but he could force it with a good shove. Instead they wandered around to the back and found an unlocked entrance at the rear. He opened the door tentatively, not sure what he'd find inside. One staff member left to guard the place, now gone insane from solitude? A clowder of feral cats, intent on protecting their territory? Or worse, snakes? A trickle of sweat slid down the back of his neck.

He flicked the switch near the door, but no lights turned on. No surprise there, as he hadn't seen a power line in the area. A place this remote would be off the grid, with a generator to produce electricity. He used the flashlight feature on his phone to look around. The air was very stale, with a hint of mustiness, but it was dry.

"Sawatdee-kah," he called out, remembering Malee's greeting at the airport.

She giggled behind him. "That's the female greeting. You say '*sawatdee-khrap.*'"

He nodded, more relieved that his greeting wasn't met by a scream or running feet, human or otherwise. Snakes wouldn't answer, of course, so he'd keep his eyes peeled. Taking a few more steps in, he turned to find Malee still standing by the door.

"Are you anxious to get home? I just need two minutes to make sure it's safe to stay here tonight."

"It's not that." Her hands were clenched at her side, and her bottom lip was being ravaged by her teeth. "I don't like the dark."

"Okay. I'll be right back." As he finished speaking, a bright flash and a loud clap of thunder overhead shook the building.

Malee shrieked and, without seeming to touch the floor, leapt to his side. "I hate storms worse," she said, her fingers digging into his arm.

Before he had time to reassure her, a torrential downpour drowned out his words of comfort. He handed her the phone with its light and quickly shut the door as water started to pour into the hallway from a broken gutter.

Tentatively wrapping an arm around Malee's shoulders, he waited for her to pull away. But evidently her fear of storms and darkness overrode her wariness of a man she'd met only a few hours before.

"Let's get to a room with windows. It won't be so

dark there," he said.

She put her arm around his waist, and for a moment a surge of protectiveness supplanted his growing desire. However, as they moved together through the gloomy, musty hotel, her hip rubbing against his thigh and her soft breast pressing into his ribs, the need to at least kiss her turned into a sharp ache.

"Have you been to the hotel before?"

Another crack of thunder had her tightening her grip on him. "Just once, four years ago, when it first opened and I was visiting my grandparents." Her voice trembled as she answered.

"Think you can direct us to the reception area?"

She pulled herself together but didn't release her hold on him, much to his surprised relief. She pointed right at the end of the hall, and in minutes, they stood in the reception area. Carefully, he opened the blinds to let in the eerie light from the storm. He retreated a few steps from the glass as the wind whipped at one of the trees on the edge of the property, throwing it to the ground and narrowly missing the SUV.

Malee shuddered, and he pulled her tighter into his arms so her face was nestled against his chest.

"I mean no harm. I'm only offering comfort," he said into the top of her hair, although the cheek rub against her silken tresses was all for him.

"Thank you. I know I shouldn't be scared, we're safe here, but…"

"If fears were logical, we wouldn't have them. Although I should warn you: if I see a snake, you're on your own." He was only half joking.

"How do you feel about spiders?"

"Why?"

"Because there's a huge one behind the reception desk."

"Poisonous?" He shuffled them a few steps away from the desk, just in case.

"I wouldn't suggest eating it to find out," she replied.

He moved a few more feet away. "Spiders and snakes don't bother you?"

"Provided I see them from far enough away, I don't mind. Until this place is thoroughly cleaned, I suggest you keep your shoes on at all times. And you'll soon find the ants and mosquitoes are the worst pests."

"I'll keep that in mind. While we're stuck inside, do you want to explore, or would you rather stay here?"

She pulled away from his chest long enough to glance outside. For being in a hot, humid environment, he oddly missed the warmth of her body, her delicate scent that filled his senses with sweetness. A small shudder shook her slight frame. "Explore. But do you mind if I hold your hand?" She stared at the floor as she asked.

With a finger under her chin, he raised her face so he could see her gorgeous brown eyes. "I wouldn't have it any other way."

Jesus, he felt alive. And it was more than just his hero complex kicking in, although that was having a field day with a frightened Malee in his arms. He wanted her near, wanted to get to know her. Her quirks, what made her laugh, what made her sad. He wanted to listen to her recite weird facts about Thailand's wonders. For the first time in his life, he wanted to delve deeper, beyond this beautiful woman's façade. The realization left him feeling oddly … vulnerable.

That was not good. Not good at all.

Chapter Three

A crack of thunder shook the hotel, and Malee stifled a scream. But no amount of willpower could stop her trembling. She forced her eyes to remain open. *I'm not trapped. I'm not in the car. I'm safe.* Wind lashed the rain against the windows and howled through the gap between the glass doors. Remembered childhood sobs tore at her heart. *Daddy! Daddy! Are you still alive?*

Strong arms wrapped around her, and she was enveloped once more against a firm, warm chest. A subtle cedar scent and the crispness of icy mint filled her senses. The softness of Caleb's cotton shirt against her cheek helped ground her in the present. His steady heartbeat was a comfort. *God, he must think me such a child.*

"You okay?" She felt as much as heard his deep voice. That was the kind of rumble she could get to like.

Forcing her arms to release him, she stepped back and ran a shaky hand down her hair. "Yes. Sorry. I'm fine. Let's check out the rest of the place."

He gave her a dubious look but took her hand in his and set off, his phone lighting the way. Everywhere they went, Caleb opened the blinds to alleviate the darkness. The storm would pass soon, and then she'd be on her way back to the village—away from this enigmatic man who, with just a hand to hold, made her feel protected. But she couldn't get attached to him just because he made her feel safe.

With a last, distant rumble of thunder, the storm abated and weak beams of late afternoon sunlight flooded the room they were in. They'd ended up in a luxury suite at the top of the building. This room looked like someone had been in it recently. A king-sized four poster bed was covered in luxurious bedding, and a small sofa sat primly against one wall. There were enough towels in the adjacent bathroom to dry a small family. The sellers had probably intended this to be the showroom they'd highlight to prospective buyers.

The rain had stopped, and Caleb threw open the French doors that led to a private terrace. Outside, everything glistened with freshness. Inside, the newly washed sunshine revealed layers of dust and cobwebs and someone's half-assed attempt to make the place look decent. With the darkness banished and the storm gone, Malee pulled in a deep breath at last … and coughed. A refreshing breeze tousled the flimsy curtains and unsettled more dust.

"I should take you home," Caleb said. His voice sounded reluctant, as if he wasn't sure he wanted to stay there alone. She wasn't sure she wanted him to, either.

It had to be inherited Thai hospitality, and not the desire to stay close to him, that had her offering, "You could stay at my grandparents' house. It has light and food and much less dust. If you don't already have asthma, this place will give it to you."

"Thanks, but I've slept in worse." He shrugged and stepped back into the hallway, leaving her no option but to follow.

"I find that hard to believe," she said as they retraced their steps to the dark, musty back entrance. As if by some unspoken signal, as soon as the light dimmed, he took her hand. His fingers wrapped around hers and sent her heart racing, but not from fear. If this guy was a mind reader, she was in serious trouble. Because after only two minutes snuggled against his chest downstairs, breathing in his manly scent, and wrapped in his hard but comforting arms, she never wanted to leave. Damn, what would it be like if they kissed?

"Why?" His question tore her from lip-lock fantasy land. They'd made it outside, and Caleb took a deep breath of the fresh air. The storm had cleared some of the humidity, but Malee knew that in less than an hour, it would be muggy and uncomfortable again. Not to mention, the mosquitoes would wake up for their nightly vampire session.

"When my agency sent me the assignment, I looked up your brother to get some background information. Your family have owned top-end hotel properties around the world for more than thirty years. No place this bad would be in your family's portfolio."

"That's true of my brother. But I left the hotel business seven years ago and started my own venture capital company. To get seed money, I worked in the oil fields in northern Alberta and slept in my truck for four months, saving every dime I earned. Let's see how your Thai mosquitoes stack up to Canadian ones. Those suckers need runways to take off."

His dedication to starting out on his own and putting in the tough graft raised her opinion of him. Which was damn uncomfortable, seeing as how she already wanted to nestle against his chest and stay there forever. Liking him as well was a nuisance.

He unlocked the door to the SUV but waited until she slid into the passenger seat before climbing behind the wheel. It was a few seconds more before he put the key in the ignition and turned it.

"I meant what I said. If you don't want to stay with my family, I'm sure someone else in the village has space. Thai people are very hospitable."

His green eyes met hers, but she couldn't read the message there. That sucked, because if it was true that ninety percent of communication was non-verbal, she was in deep trouble with this man. Her whole livelihood depended on being able to understand what people actually meant, not merely what they said.

"I'll be fine here. I need some time alone." He pulled his gaze from hers then turned the vehicle around and started back down the mountain. His rejection stung. But she couldn't blame him. She'd been unprofessional at best. At worst, an annoying drama queen. Her heart chilled.

A hundred new waterfalls had formed since they'd driven by earlier. The road was slick with mud, and a few rocks and branches were strewn across the path. When they came across a larger tree in their way, Caleb put the vehicle in park and got out.

"I can help," Malee offered, her hand on the door.

"No, I've got this."

She cranked the SUV's air conditioning to high as he bent over to pick up the tree. His trousers strained against his backside, revealing a firm, rounded butt. The Thai woman in her said to look away, but somehow the message never made it to her eyes. He was her boss; she shouldn't be fantasizing about him. Then he threw the fallen tree down into the ravine. His biceps bulged, and the muscles in his back rippled under his now sweat-soaked white shirt. He might be her employer, but she was all woman.

It didn't hurt to look, right? Nothing could come of this weird, tingly attraction. He was good-looking and built to withstand a hurricane. Any woman would feel safe, special even, in his arms. But that was all it was, all it could ever be—a temporary physical fascination. She longed for a true partnership, where she and her future spouse would work side by side, maybe not in business, but at least in the home. Cooking, cleaning, raising the kids—three, if she was lucky—decorating, going on outings … they'd all be done together. A true family. A bond that would see her children secure in life, without phobias that kept them on medication for months at a time. Not the sort of thing she could even imagine with the man in front of her. Caleb didn't come across as the type to appreciate simple domesticity.

Plus, the man she eventually married would have to realize that family came first with Malee and always would. There had been no warmth in his tone when Caleb spoke of his father or brother. And she could sense the restlessness in his soul. He was the proverbial rolling stone. Her heart was in Thailand. She couldn't be content anywhere else.

Except now that she was back, she didn't seem to fit in here, either. The disquiet that she'd thought was homesickness for her native land hadn't abated. But it was early days. Surely in a few more months, she'd feel at home, be able to settle and look to the future. She dismissed the feeling that she'd been gone too long. That she was too westernized now to live in a small, remote village and marry a rice farmer. Not that there was anything wrong with marrying a rice farmer.

Coming home had been her dream for so long, she just couldn't believe it had finally come true. The line from *Finding Nemo*, when all the fish from the dentist's tank were finally in the ocean, kept flitting through her brain: *Now what?*

Caleb had a few more scratches on his arm when he returned to the car. One was bleeding slightly, and Malee wet a handkerchief with the bottle of water she kept in her bag and dabbed at it before the blood could drip and stain his clothes.

"Do you have a temperamental cat at home?" He said he didn't have a girlfriend, but maybe a casual hook-up had been a little too aggressive. The idea made her queasy.

"I was rock climbing when I got the message that my brother ... wasn't able to make this trip."

"Do you often climb rocks?" She tried to equate risking life with having fun and came up blank. That was one gene of her father's she hadn't inherited. He'd enjoyed dangerous sports as well—free diving, hang gliding, caving … not to mention reckless driving, which had cost him his life and almost taken hers.

"Every chance I get. Work keeps me insanely busy. But when the office gets too much, I grab my gear and head out. It makes me feel alive to hang off the side of a cliff with only my fingers and toes holding on."

Malee barely repressed a shudder. "Really? It takes being near death to make you feel alive? Breathing does it for me." She added a laugh so it didn't sound like she was dissing his favorite sport, as crazy as it was.

His low chuckle filled the car, and a shiver rippled over her skin. She turned the air conditioning back down.

They edged another half-kilometer down the road until Caleb swore under his breath. Malee looked over to him and then out the windscreen. She'd had her eyes closed, her fingernails embedded in the soft leather seat, for the last few minutes, not wanting to see them go over the edge. Ahead, the road had completely disappeared, leaving only a gaping hole.

They were stranded.

For the foreseeable future.

Just the two of them.

***

Caleb got out and examined the area where the road should have been. A five-meter section of land had slid down the mountainside, sweeping trees and large boulders with it. The side where the road had disappeared was a sheer drop for at least fifty meters. After that, it was dense jungle, so he couldn't see the bottom. He grabbed a stick from the edge and tested the soil consistency. Could they make the trek across? The wood sank easily into the earth. It would be too treacherous; their footing could give way and they'd fall.

Malee had gotten out of the car and stared down into the ravine, her trembling visible. She kicked a rock, and it went tumbling over the edge. "We're stranded." The hoarseness in her voice betrayed her anxiety.

"I'll take you back to the resort. If I can find some rope, I can make it across to get help."

Her shaking increased. "It's too dangerous."

He assessed the slope again. She was right. No point killing himself his first day in the country.

"We'll go back to the hotel and try again tomorrow. You told the guy at the store where we stopped that we were coming up here, so people will be looking for us." At the very least, the property owners would be coming next week to conclude negotiations. He wished now he hadn't put the meeting off for so long. How was he to know he'd be stranded … with his beautiful translator? Maybe there was a silver lining to this disaster.

Malee nodded and returned to the SUV. That put the question of where to sleep tonight to rest. By the time they got back to the resort, the sun would be low in the sky. If there was one thing Caleb knew about the tropics, pitch blackness wouldn't be long behind. And he was with a woman who wasn't too keen on the dark.

"I shouldn't have insisted on seeing the property today," he said by way of apology when he'd parked again—a little farther from the trees in case there was another storm.

Was it so wrong he was secretly glad that Malee was still here with him? His body had been at war for the past two hours. Part of him needed to be alone, or at least away from Malee, to regain his equilibrium. It had to be exhaustion, and a recent dearth of female companionship, that accounted for his burgeoning obsession with his Thai translator. The other part of him wanted to keep her near, discover her secrets, taste her light brown skin, sink himself into her warmth, and forget the looming corporate restructuring on his horizon.

"It's not your fault." She shrugged as she got out of the vehicle and immediately disappeared.

He raced around and came to skidding halt when he saw her sitting beside the car in an enormous mud puddle. Reaching out a hand to help her up, he thought he'd braced himself, but as soon as Malee put her hand in his, he slipped and fell into the mud beside her. The splash he created splattered mud on her top and face. Expecting a hiss of disapproval, he was surprised when she burst into laughter.

"Welcome to Thailand," she finally managed to say when she got control of herself.

"So far, it's been a very interesting country. It is definitely different from my other business trips," he said. "I usually leave the mud bath for the last day."

Her face was alight with joy, until she looked up at the sky and a hint of fear clouded her chocolate-brown eyes. The answering clenching of his stomach wasn't a welcome development either. "We'd better get cleaned up. We have about half an hour of daylight left."

She flipped over to her hands and knees and Caleb had to briefly close his eyes as her firm ass put him in mind of other activities. Halfway out of the puddle, Malee's hands lost traction and she ended up face first in the mud. He stifled a laugh, only to have the same thing happen to him. By the time they'd made it to the grass, there wasn't a clean spot on them.

He risked standing, then helped Malee to her feet. She kept hold of his hand and tugged him around the back of the hotel. Rather than head for the door where they'd gained entrance earlier, she kept walking down a cement path. The sound of crashing water became louder until she pushed aside a banana leaf and they stood next to a small waterfall.

She let go of his hand and walked around the pebbled edge of the pond before wading in. "It's deep enough if you want to jump," she said. "Just aim for the middle."

That was too good an offer to refuse. Besides, jumping in would get the mud off quicker. "Holy shit!" he yelled as soon as he broke the surface of the water. "It's freezing." His balls were attempting to retreat into his body.

Malee laughed again. It wasn't a coquettish titter aimed to seduce. Her mirth was genuine and pure. "Sorry, didn't I warn you?"

She waded in up to her waist and disappeared under the water. He could see her scrub at her face and hair. When she surfaced again, her teeth started to chatter. She swam toward a rock and hauled herself up. The mud was gone, but the water made her clothes cling to her shapely body. Thank God the water was so cold—it numbed his reaction to her. Or so he hoped. There'd be no hiding his erection in these wet clothes.

Malee strode over to a stack of plastic pails, kicked them over, then jumped back. "Good. I didn't have to evict anything." She separated the buckets and passed two to him. "We're going to need water up at the hotel." She waded back into the freezing pool and filled her two pails before he could move.

No water, no electricity, a loaf of bread and a few other basic provisions that they'd luckily thought to pick up in the village ... it was going to be a hell of a camping trip. At least he had a few changes of clothes. Malee only had those she wore and they were soaking wet. He waded into the pool and filled the buckets she'd given him before he began to envisage ways of warming her.

She was already halfway up the path back to the hotel before he'd scrambled from the water. "Be sure to check for leeches when you change your clothes," she called over her shoulder.

Wonderful. So far, the only thing to recommend this place was the sight of Malee's firm ass climbing the stairs ahead of him. They couldn't put that on a hotel brochure.

He caught up with her on the grassed path back to the hotel. She carried the water with little effort and seemed only slightly out of breath. She was tougher than she appeared. His respect for her doubled. *What if I'd been stuck with someone like my mother?* The shudder that wracked his body this time wasn't from the cold.

"You're going to be uncomfortable in those wet clothes," he said. "I'll lend you something."

She blinked as though shuttering her thoughts. "I have a dress in my bag. I was going to put in on at the airport before I met you. But the bus was full and I couldn't get on and then, well, I ended up being late… But I will borrow a T-shirt to sleep in, if that's okay."

Malee in his T-shirt, sleeping nearby. Yeah, that was more than okay.

"Sure."

As soon as they entered the hotel, Malee left the pails of water by the door and headed straight for the clearly marked supply room, muttering, "Thank God," under her breath as she reached for a lantern next to a bunch of small gas cylinders stacked on a shelf.

With an ease that had to be borne of practice, she checked over the gas canister, attached it to a lantern, and lit it with a nearby package of matches. The dark, dank room flooded with light. She lit another one and handed it to him. "Can you bring the buckets to the kitchen? I'm hoping there's still a propane stove there where I can boil the water to purify it."

She'd taken charge, and he let her for the moment. He may not like being told what to do, but he wasn't so stupid that he didn't recognize when someone else was more qualified for a task.

He followed her down a couple more hallways until they entered a small but well-equipped kitchen. The stainless-steel appliances were dusty but otherwise clean. Malee quickly found a hotplate and attached another gas cylinder to it. After a couple of tries, it finally lit. He left her going through the cupboards and went to retrieve the water they'd abandoned by the back door. From the banging and clattering, Malee was seeing what was available to use. She was still investigating when he brought in her bag and his from the car.

"You need to get out of those cold, wet clothes," he said. Her lips were blue, and she was shivering.

She nodded and picked up a gas lamp and her bag, hesitating at the door. "Which room are you going to sleep in? Or are you planning to bed down in the car?"

"The SUV is too small to stretch out. Why don't you use the room we checked out earlier? I'm pretty sure there's a similar suite next door for me."

"Okay." Still, she hesitated. "Do you mind coming with me? It's just the dark hallways and shadows and stuff…"

"It will be my pleasure." He snagged his suitcase, grasped her hand, and led her back to the top of the hotel. While Malee changed, Caleb checked out the neighboring room, leaving the door open in case she called out. After removing the dust covers from the furniture, he opened the patio doors to let in some fresh air, careful to keep the mosquito net pulled across the doorway.

Frogs and crickets filled the evening air with their chatter. A gentle breeze rustled the leaves of the jungle foliage, and the faint sound of tumbling water provided a soothing backdrop. Despite the lack of luxury, or maybe because of it, stress fell from him in waves. There'd be no urgent phone calls or emails. No one demanding a meeting or begging him to invest in their latest hare-brained scheme. Just him, a beautiful woman, and a night filled with stars.

He was so intent on enjoying the moment that he didn't hear Malee approach. Or it could have been her lack of footwear, since she held a pair of heeled shoes in her hand. Her hair had been combed through and pulled back off her face, which was clean of makeup. In the moonlight, her dark eyes smiled at him, pulling his own lips upward. A light blue dress with short cap sleeves came to her knees. It would have looked entirely professional, except her hard nipples jutted against the silk fabric. He would've bet his last dollar she wasn't wearing underwear. The parts of him that didn't clench swelled in hopeful anticipation. How was a guy supposed to function, knowing he was one piece of cloth away from paradise?

But while she stood beside him, so tiny compared to him, and technically his employee for the next week, he knew he had to keep his hands, lips, and other body parts in check.

"Shall we dine?" he asked, offering his arm. They had only the few provisions he'd picked up in the village, but he hadn't eaten in hours. It was going to be a lean few days until they were rescued. Tomorrow, he'd see if there was any way to traverse the missing bit of road. Maybe if he climbed above the landslide, they could make it down the other side. But chances were high there were other slips along the roadway. The last thing they needed was to be stranded without even a building for shelter.

"Don't you want to change first?" Her gaze slid down his body, and she bit down on her lower lip.

He'd pretty much steam-dried his clothes walking up

the hill behind her, and with her hot gaze and obvious interest, he was more worried about catching fire than freezing. "I'll be fine for now."

She nodded and put on her shoes, which made her a few inches taller but still nowhere near his height. They detoured to the wine cellar on the way back to the kitchen. Caleb could have wept happy tears when he saw that a few bottles had been left behind. Whether they'd be drinkable or not was another thing.

They ate at a small table in the kitchen. The bread was fresh and delicious, the spiced chicken noodle salad incredible, and the wine drinkable. Five-star dining on a Happy Meal budget. Malee boiled some water so they could safely brush their teeth, and then they headed upstairs again.

He hadn't slept in thirty-six hours, but a weird energy zapped through him. "I'll get you a T-shirt," he said before disappearing into his room. He gave her the first one he grabbed from his bag and then waited until Malee had shut her door behind her. As he got ready for bed, he could hear her doing the same next door. He found it strangely erotic. Had she slipped on his shirt yet? How far down her thighs did it come? When she bent over, did it reveal her firm ass? Did the cotton brush against her nipples, peaking them like they'd been through most of dinner? Had she been cold then, or turned on?

He lay in bed, contemplating a trek back down to the waterfall to cool his overheated blood, when there was a loud crack of thunder above the hotel, followed by another torrential downpour. If these violent storms kept up, they'd be lucky to leave by the end of the month.

A flash of lightening lit the room the same second as another clap of thunder boomed, bouncing off the walls and shaking the bed. He should check on Malee. She was probably huddled in the fetal position, scared stiff. Throwing off the covers, he relit the gas lantern so he could see if anything had invaded his boxers before he put them on. He'd taken two steps toward his suitcase when his bedroom door was flung open.

Wide-eyed, Malee stood there, her light held before her, her hair disheveled, his T-shirt clinging to her curves like it couldn't touch her enough. Her eyes searched the bed at first, and then landed on him, standing naked in the middle of the room. "Can I sleep with you tonight?" she asked.

Chapter Four

This must be my day for seeing people naked. But finding Caleb in the buff was a damn sight more enticing than catching her grandparents. Despite her panicked state, she couldn't help noticing he was at half-mast. Had he been thinking of her? Dinner had been torture, sitting across from him, wearing nothing but her dress, feeling scandalous. Who knew underwear provided such protection? Her previous boyfriend had been such a disappointing lover that she hadn't missed sex all that much. Then Caleb, without even making any advances, had her thinking about things she ought not to want.

He's your boss, girl. But that hadn't stopped her from asking if she could sleep with him. His eyes widened at her question, and she didn't dare look lower to see if there was any other reaction.

She cleared her throat. "I mean, can I stay in your room? I can sleep on the floor or the sofa." She glanced at the couch. If it had had a dust cover, it obviously hadn't been put on soon enough. Even in this light, it was clearly covered in a fine layer of dirt.

She shivered as another roar of thunder drowned out Caleb's reply.

"Get in the bed, Malee," he repeated as he pulled on

a pair of underwear. "It's big enough, and I won't be able to sleep if I know you're uncomfortable."

Like she was going to be comfortable sleeping in the same bed as him.

"I'm sure the storm will pass soon. I'll go back to my own room…"

He strode over to her, scooped her in his arms, and dropped her on the bed on the side he'd just exited. The sheets were still warm from his body, and she could smell a faint trace of his woodsy cologne on the pillow.

"I can't remember the last time I slept," he said. "I promise not to ravage you in the night. Now relax if you can, and tomorrow we'll find a way out of here." He turned the lantern down low, placed it on the bedside table next to her, and climbed in on the other side of the bed. "Would it make you feel better if we put a wall of pillows between us?"

"No. I trust you." Aside from a few hot looks, Caleb hadn't made any advances or suggestive comments. Even when he'd held her during the earlier storm, he hadn't taken advantage of the situation.

They both lay on their backs, staring at the ceiling. The storm raged above them, but her fear had taken a backseat to her awareness of the man next to her. News flash: sexual tension discovered as a cure for astraphobia.

"Does it often storm like this? The sky was clear before we ate. I was admiring the stars." His voice was soft, intimate, even though they were discussing the weather.

"It's almost the end of monsoon season. Another few

weeks and the weather will be drier."

"This time of year must be hell for you." There was no censure in his voice, just compassion. He might be the one man in the world who didn't treat her like a freak for still having childish fears at twenty-five. "Have you always been scared of the dark and storms?"

She turned her head to look at him. He'd crossed his arms above his head and although his eyes were closed, she sensed he was as alert as ever. It wasn't a story she liked to tell, but the man had held her hand all day and let her into his bed.

"When I was eight, I was in the car with my father during a bad storm. We were late because I hadn't wanted to leave my grandparents' place to go home to Chiang Mai." She swallowed down the inevitable guilt. Her mother had reassured her over and over again it wasn't her fault. Still... Her heart pounded in her chest, and a trickle of sweat slid down her forehead. Another rumble of thunder filled the room, and she fisted her hands to stop the tremors. Somehow, Caleb's calm, even breathing next to her helped steady her nerves.

She hauled in a deep breath so she could tell him the rest. "My father took a turn too fast. The car left the road and tumbled down the side of the mountain. I was strapped in and mostly unhurt, but by the time the rescuers found us, almost three days had passed, and my dad had died."

A small gasp came from his side of the bed. "Your father was alive at first?"

"Yes. He was coherent for the first day, but as the pain got worse, he phased in and out of consciousness. I learned later his lung had been punctured. He had internal injuries and slowly bled to death."

Caleb's eyes opened then, but he made no move to touch her. She was both relieved and disappointed. "Why did it take them so long to find you?"

"The car was upside down and in the deep jungle. It was pitch black most of the time and the storm didn't let up. The darkness and thunder make me relive those days—hearing Dad cry out in pain, then eventually not make any noise at all … wondering if we'd ever be found…"

Caleb turned on his side to face her. "If I went through something like that, I'm sure I'd hate the dark and storms as well."

"It's nice of you to say, but I'm a grown woman now. I should be able to get over this."

"Malee, never apologize for feeling things. It's the people without emotions who are monsters."

"Thank you," she said past a lump in her throat. Previous boyfriends, even some of her family, had criticized her for her fears. To have a virtual stranger acknowledge that she had a right to be traumatized meant more than she could say.

He reached out a hand but hesitated before he touched her. "I was going to move a piece of hair off your face, but I remembered it's disrespectful to touch a Thai person's head," he said.

"I don't mind. I lived in England for so long, sometimes I feel more British than Thai."

Gently he lifted the strand of hair and then smoothed it down the back of her head. "I'm about to fall asleep.

But if you're frightened in the night, don't hesitate to wake me."

She nodded, although she knew she wouldn't. Just having another warm—scratch that, *hot*—body near had already lightened her fears. Sleep lurked like a shadow on her shoulder. A sense of peace washed over her. And that was odd, because the last thing she expected to feel in bed with Caleb Doyle was peaceful.

His eyes drifted closed, his hand still lingering on her shoulder.

When she woke, the birds were chirping, and sunlight streamed into the room. She was spooning Caleb, her hand resting on his lower abdomen, her bare thighs pressed against his. His breathing was deep and even. Poor man. He was exhausted, and she'd not only invaded his bed but suctioned herself to him.

She eased away and silently slipped from the bed and the room before she did something stupid.

***

Caleb held back a groan as Malee left the bed. Her soft body pressed against his had been the most exquisite torture. Had her hand slipped another centimeter south, she'd have discovered just how much he wanted to roll over, remove his shirt from her body, and taste every inch of her skin. If they didn't find a way back to civilization today, he'd have to see a doctor about an erection lasting longer than four hours.

On the plus side, he'd had an excellent sleep and was ready to face the day and its challenges. He waited until he heard Malee leave the room next door. She must have dressed and would be headed to the kitchen to see if there was anything to eat. They'd saved some bread from yesterday, but there wasn't a lot else. A few items had been left behind when the hotel had been abandoned, but he had no idea if they'd still be edible.

He flung back the sheet, grabbed a change of clothes, a little bar of soap, and a towel, and headed back to the waterfall. As soon as he washed, he'd help Malee with breakfast. Hopefully with her local knowledge, she could direct them out of here. If he could send a message, he'd hire a helicopter to get them back to the airport if he had to.

His brain was full of escape plans when he heard a faint splash ahead of him. Perhaps the pool at the base of the falls was the local watering hole for the animals in the area. Were there still tigers in this part of Asia? Maybe it was a domesticated elephant and they could ride their way back to the village. He laughed to himself. Was jungle fever a real thing? Did it start with weird imaginings?

Carefully, he moved a palm frond and froze. All the air fled his lungs, but he was too mesmerized to breathe in. Malee stood in the water up to mid-thigh, completely naked. Her small hands rubbed a bar of soap over her body. God, he so wanted to be that bar of soap right now. He knew he should take a step back and leave her to her washing, but he couldn't look away.

The female form was not new to him. He'd had his fair share of women over the years, but nothing he'd ever seen before was as erotic as this.

Her sun-kissed skin glistened in the water. Her dark nipples were hard from the cold water, jutting from her chest and begging him to take them in his mouth to warm them. When she raised her hands to run the soap through her hair, any remaining blood that had been circulating throughout his body headed straight for his cock.

She splashed her way into deeper water to wash off the soap, allowing him to make a strategic retreat. Malee would be so embarrassed if she knew he'd seen her. Then again, she had found him naked last night when she'd come to his room.

He'd get a start on breakfast and head down to the water when he was sure it was clear of a certain gorgeous woman.

Climbing the stairs back to the hotel was agony with his erection straining against his jeans. As he crested the hill, he noticed a small concrete building set back from the main hotel, and walked over to check it out. There was a padlock on the door, but with the tire iron from the SUV it broke easily enough. Given that his idiot brother had paid a ten-thousand-dollar deposit to secure his bid on the property, Caleb didn't feel bad about a little vandalism.

He opened the door carefully in case anything inside suddenly wanted to be outside. Although if it had been locked tight for two years, all he was likely to find were bones. Two large generators and a twenty-gallon drum of diesel were the only things within. All the instructions were in Thai, but machines were machines no matter the language, so after checking to make sure everything was still connected where it should be, he pressed the start button.

Nothing, not even a splutter.

"According to the sign, you need to flip the red switch over here," Malee said, startling him. She was dressed in her shorts and T-shirt from yesterday, her neatly braided hair still dripping at the tip. He blinked to rid his brain of the image of her in the water, but it didn't work. Jesus, was he going to see her naked body every time he looked at her? That would be awkward.

She flipped the switch and he tried the start button once more. It spluttered a few times but didn't take. The fuel had probably destabilized. If they could find a way out of here, it would be a waste of time to try and get it working. A weird sense of loss filled him. Why the hell did he want to stay in the middle of nowhere?

Malee shifted her weight from one foot to the other, looking longingly at the generator. Then her gaze landed on his towel and a fierce blush infused her skin.

"I'll have a look at it again after I've had a wash. I was headed toward the waterfall when I saw the building and decided to investigate." He looked her straight in the eye.

"I, uh, was just there. Don't worry, I left some water for you." Her laugh held a lingering note of embarrassment. "Actually, I'm surprised you're up already. I figured after your long flight, the time difference, and yesterday's events, you'd sleep until noon." Her eyes once more flitted to his towel. "I'll find something for breakfast and meet you in the kitchen when you're done." She headed back toward the hotel, hesitating briefly before entering the darkened hallway.

But she squared her shoulders and stepped into the building and out of sight.

He hurried to the waterfall, shedding his clothes as he went. He cannon-balled into the pool, yelling out as he entered the frigid water. He swam around for a few minutes, enjoying the bizarre freedom of being naked outdoors and knowing he wouldn't become an internet meme or the front page of a tabloid. So far, he'd managed to keep his personal life private. But a man with his bank account always had to be careful about whom he trusted with secrets—like his desire for a certain Thai translator. Although that was becoming less a secret and more an internal battle.

Floating on his back, he stared at the blue sky. Yes, he was stuck at the hotel, cut off from the rest of the world. But for once, he didn't care. Was it wrong to hope they couldn't get back to the village for a couple of days?

**

Malee tightened her grip on the spoon. It wasn't much of a breakfast, but at least it was something. She'd found some rice that was still good and a can of tuna, and she'd managed to spice it up with a few herbs and peppers from the kitchen garden at the back of the hotel. The vegetable plot was overrun with weeds and nearly indistinguishable from the surrounding grass. Four years ago, during a holiday to visit her grandparents, she'd visited the hotel with her chef mother and had been shown around. Otherwise, she'd never have known the garden existed or managed to locate the hidden pantry.

She'd found some salt cod and had put that on soak, in case they were still here tonight.

Did she want to still be here tonight? Of course, she didn't. She needed to check in on her grandparents and write to her mother and sit around waiting for her life to resume. Or she could use the time she had to sell Caleb on the resort. Yes, they were off to a shaky start, but if she could get him to see the potential... But at what risk? She was already drawn to him like a butterfly to flowers. If they were isolated much longer, something was bound to give. Like her ability to stay in the kitchen knowing he was frolicking naked in the water just a few meters away.

She'd hoped the chilly water would cool her lust this morning. Instead, she'd imagined it was Caleb's hands caressing her body as she ran the soap over her skin. Would it be so bad to indulge in a little holiday romance? Her body heated and she closed her eyes for a second, remembering the scene she'd walked in on last night in his bedroom. She had a feeling it wouldn't be hard to convince him to indulge in a little passion until they were rescued.

It was the antithesis of what a good Thai woman would do. She was trying to integrate back into the society, not alienate herself further. But here, cut off from the rest of the world, who would know? The lure of one last Western fling before she leashed her passions and resumed the guise of a demure woman was so tempting.

Damn. What if he didn't have any condoms? A fling was one thing, an unplanned pregnancy another. Then the image of Caleb naked last night streaked through her brain. No man that good-looking would travel without protection. Would he?

Caleb's footsteps and a muttered curse as he knocked a pail of water against the wall gave her a moment to compose herself. Still, when he entered the kitchen, his muscles bulging with the weight of the water he carried, his hair damp and unruly, and his T-shirt stretched tight across his body, she could've wept for the beauty of his form. Then his green eyes, lit with warmth, met hers, and her ovaries went into alert mode.

"It smells great in here. If I'm hallucinating from hunger, don't tell me," he said.

"I found a few things in the pantry that were still edible. You don't have any food allergies, do you?" I would be just her luck to poison him with her first meal.

"No allergies. I'm pretty easy to please."

Her face flamed. *Good to know.*

"It's almost ready. After breakfast, I guess we'll need to find out if there's a way out of here, right?" She stirred the pot one last time then grabbed two plates and dished out the meal. It did smell good, and her stomach rumbled.

Caleb picked up the plates, and she grabbed the cutlery. Instead of eating at one of the stainless-steel work benches, he led her outside, where he'd set up a table and chairs on the front deck. The view was spectacular—lush green mountains, a few terraced with rice paddies, the rest left to nature—and the air clean and fresh after last night's thunderstorm. A few clouds were gathering over a nearby hill, but for the moment, they appeared harmless.

"Your family will be worried about you," Caleb said. He'd already cleared half his plate. The man must have been starving, having shared his dinner with her last night.

"Probably. But at least they know where we were headed." Unlike her father, who had once disappeared for five days to explore some nearby caves without telling anyone. He'd been trapped there by rising water, leaving her mother frantic. Malee could still remember the scene when her father strolled into the house unharmed and her normally placid mother lashed out at him for his insensitivity. She'd learned a valuable lesson in what to look for in a future husband that day.

"Is there any other access, aside from the road?" Caleb asked.

"There's a bare spot at the top of the mountain that was used as a helicopter landing pad during construction. But my family's chopper is in for repairs, so that rules out that form of rescue." Her lips twitched, and she lost the battle to maintain a serious expression.

He laughed, and a couple of birds that had hovered nearby, hoping for a tidbit to eat, flew off.

"That was excellent," he said, rubbing his flat stomach. "If you cook that well with just a few meager ingredients, I'd love to see what you could do with a stocked pantry."

"Thank you. My mother is a chef. She taught me to cook. I was hoping that if you reopened the hotel, she could get a job here and be closer to her parents." Malee looked at him through her lashes to judge his reaction.

"I can't open a hotel no one can get to," he replied.

The hard edge to his voice stopped her from attempting to persuade him further. "Of course. I'll be ready to go in half an hour. I just need to wash up the dishes. If we can't get away, we don't want to be overrun by ants."

He nodded and followed her back into the hotel. Caleb went upstairs to grab his bag and hers. As she tidied the kitchen, a distant rumble of thunder sent an eerie chill down her spine.

Please, for once, let the storm just pass over.

Her answer was a sudden darkening, quickly followed by a torrential downpour.

She wanted to scream for Caleb, but what was the use? In a few hours, he'd be gone from her life.

Chapter Five

Jesus. Storms moved in fast here. Twenty minutes ago, he'd noticed a few dark clouds on the horizon. Then with one distant clap of thunder, the heavens opened. No way could he force a petrified Malee into the SUV for a trek down the mountain. He could go himself, but it didn't sit well with him to leave her here on her own, terrified. They'd have to wait it out.

After zipping his suitcase closed, he hurried out of the room in search of his translator. He found her in the kitchen, huddled in the corner, her hands over her ears as another clap of thunder shook the building. Her frightened eyes met his. How could she bear to live here if this was a daily occurrence?

He crouched down in front of her. "What can I do to help?"

"Hold me?"

Her eyes had returned to the floor, but when he pulled her up and into his arms, her gaze briefly met his. If he didn't have a hero complex before, he would by the end of their time together. She made him feel needed, worthy, strong. Wanted for more than his money or a good time. She snuggled against him, and he inhaled deeply of her soap-and-flowers scent.

"What do you do when I'm not around?" he asked. The idea of Malee seeking comfort in another man's arms bothered him. It was an annoying flicker of jealousy. He was here to do a job and then leave. No attachments. He was far too restless to settle down with one woman. And his parent's marriage had shown him what happened when two people were only interested in their own happiness.

"I have some tablets that take the edge off the anxiety. But I left them at my grandparents' house." Another boom of thunder reverberated through the room, and Malee hugged him tighter.

"Until I can get you back home, I'll be your Xanax."

They stood in silence for a while as the storm raged above them. He ran his hands up and down her back but ventured no lower. Oddly, her presence in his arms was a soothing balm to him as well. The itch that spurred him on to do crazy things almost disappeared.

"You smell like Canada to me." Her voice was muffled against his chest, her warm breath curling around his pectoral muscles through his thin T-shirt.

"Like unwashed hockey equipment and mosquito repellent?"

She laughed like she had yesterday in the mud—full-body mirth that drew an answering response from him. Two things hit him simultaneously. First, he'd been able to make her laugh in the middle of a terrifying thunderstorm. And second, it was the most beautiful sound he'd ever heard. Hearing it again had just become his mission in life.

"No," she said once she'd managed to stop laughing. "Like tall trees and fresh air."

"Canada does have plenty of those things. What

would you say Thailand smells like?"

Another clap of thunder, although a little quieter, delayed her answer. She pulled in a deep breath that thrust her full breasts harder against his upper abdomen. Lust washed through him and for a moment, he forgot his question.

"Rotting fruit and mud?" she replied.

"I think it's tropical flowers with a touch of lemongrass." That's what she smelled like, and his thoughts of Thailand would forever be centered on this woman.

She nodded her head, her cheek rubbing against his chest. "Okay, I'd agree with that."

They stood for a few more minutes in silence. Her soft breathing, the warmth of her body pressed against his, and the tickle of her hair on his stubble-covered jaw infused him with a peace he'd never experienced before. How could holding a traumatized woman bring him such contentment?

The thunder rumbled again, more distant this time, but the rain didn't lessen. Malee eased out of his arms.

"Thank you," she said, her eyes once more on the floor.

"Hey, I thought we agreed you'd look me in the eye."

Finally, she raised her eyes to his, a faint blush staining her cheeks. "I'm so embarrassed."

"Would it help if I told you that I actually enjoy having you in my arms? And not in a creepy way," he quickly added. Okay, so maybe watching her wash this morning was slightly creepy, but he wasn't going to revisit that experience with her so close.

"Do you want to leave now?" She glanced out the kitchen window. It was still bucketing down even though the thunder had moved on.

"We'd better wait for the rain to stop. The road is bad enough as it is."

He didn't need to be holding her to know she heaved a huge sigh of relief. "So, what shall we do until then?"

"Are you up for a little exploring? There are a few more rooms we haven't checked out. According to the floor plans, there's supposed to be a lounge and a dining room somewhere." He hadn't been in enough Thai hotels to know if this one's eclectic floor plan was typical or not.

"I believe it's on the second floor. We skipped that one when we were searching yesterday."

Without waiting for a reply, she grabbed a lantern with one hand, took his hand in the other, and proceeded out of the room. Her slim fingers rubbed against the back of his hand. Did she have any idea what her touch did to him? It contrasted with the desire ricocheting throughout his body, and a strange peace and a flood of wellbeing soothed his soul.

The central stairs were dark, but Malee didn't hesitate. And when she released his hand to fling open the double doors on the second floor, not even the loss of her touch could stop his gasp of surprise as he viewed the room.

This was what he'd expected of a Thai resort, albeit with a lot less dust and cobwebs. Sturdy teak furniture was placed in cozy groupings throughout the room. A wall of windows that appeared to cantilever open spanned the far side of the space. At the moment, all that could be seen was a deluge of water pouring from the sky like an overturned bucket. But he could imagine that on a clear day, the view would be magnificent. Now he understood why this room was on the second and not the ground floor: the elevation allowed the vista to be unencumbered by the trees surrounding the property.

At the far end, tables and chairs were set up as an informal dining room. Through an intricately carved latticed screen, he could just glimpse a more formal eating space beyond.

"How come there's so much stuff left behind? This looks like good-quality furniture." He ran a finger along the wide wooden armrest of a sofa, a bit mystified by the thick metal chains resting on it.

"From what I remember my grandparents saying, there was always hope the hotel would be reopened. And it took so much effort just to get the furniture here, the owners didn't want to cart it all out. I'm sure the purchase price includes all this stuff."

"Why is this one chained? Does it have a habit of wandering off?"

Malee laughed again. "No." She pointed at the ceiling. "It hangs from those hooks. Stops ants and other creepy crawlies from getting on it."

"I vote we chill out here until the storm clears. Unless seeing the rain through the windows distresses you too much."

"No. This is good. But it's rather filthy. If you don't mind waiting a bit, I can give it a quick clean," she said.

"*We* can give it a quick clean. I'll bring a bucket of

water up from downstairs. You see if you can find some cleaning stuff. Okay?"

"Aye, aye, captain," she said with a jaunty salute, her British accent even more pronounced. She grabbed the lantern and raced from the room.

He fetched the water and returned before Malee. To let some fresh air into the stale room, he opened the glass doors. An overhang from the roof stopped the rain from entering, but the terrace had huge cracks in the cement. Not only did it appear too dangerous to stand on, but it was probably leaking into the rooms below as well.

How the hell had Ian been suckered into putting down a bid deposit on this place? It was barely worth the ten grand he'd already paid, never mind the million they were asking. His brother had always been conservative in business. Had the stress of seeing their father's company spiraling downward made him reckless? Or was there fraud involved here?

Whatever the reason, Caleb would get to the bottom of it. If there was even a hint of misrepresentation, he'd unleash super-lawyer Harrison on the owners. He might not be best buddies with his brother, but no one scammed a Doyle. The meeting with the sellers next week—or whenever the hell they escaped this place—was not going to be the amicable one they imagined.

Malee banged through the doors, laden with items. She held a bucket with cleaning supplies in one hand, the lantern in the other, and a couple of folded sheets and a feather duster under one arm.

The rain hadn't let up one iota, so they got to work. He beat some of the dust from the sofa cushions out the windows, while Malee wiped everything down, spritzed some lemon-scented polish, and rubbed it in. Within the hour, the room was habitable and a damn sight more comfortable than any other place in the hotel.

"I think we should hang the sofa," he said, hands on his hips, surveying their hard work. Sitting on a suspended sofa appealed to his inner child.

"Um, how? I haven't seen a ladder around."

He hadn't either. But it wasn't very high. "Climb on my shoulders. I'll lift it, while you hook it on the ceiling anchors."

She glanced from the sofa to his shoulder and then the floor. "Climb on you?"

"Yeah." He handed her the end of the chain then crouched down so she could climb up.

"I'm not sure about this," she said, but flung one leg over his shoulder. Her tanned thighs grazed his cheeks, putting him in mind of other activities.

As he straightened, she ran her fingers through his hair, tugging lightly on the strands. As she reached higher to place the chain on the ceiling hooks, her crotch rubbed against the back of his head and her thighs tightened against his face.

This had seemed like a good idea at the time. Now it just might kill him.

***

Malee squinted with one eye open as she attached the last hook to the ceiling to hold up the sofa. It wasn't the height that bothered her. It was the undignified position on Caleb's shoulders that made her want to squirm. Evidently there were still some Thai sensibilities left in her.

"That's it. You can let me down now," she said, expecting him to squat down so she could climb off the way she'd gotten on.

Instead he put his hands on her waist, swung her around to his front, and slid her down his body until she stood before him. His gaze blazed into hers, and the air around them crackled with awareness. This was lightening without the thunder.

Finally, Caleb tore his eyes from hers and examined the sofa. It hung half a meter off the floor. Its thick pillows looked inviting, but despite his attempts to rid them of dust, they still looked sneeze inducing. Malee took a step back and shivered. His hands dropped from her waist. How could she feel a chill when it had to be thirty degrees Celsius, even with the window open and the rain outside?

"Shall we test it?" he asked.

He pushed down on the arm as though to check that the hooks would hold. Thankfully, or not, considering the rising attraction between them, they held firm. The sofa was long enough that they could both stretch out, side by side. And that was an image she did not need in her brain. Especially given the way she'd woken up this morning.

"I brought some clean-ish sheets to throw on top."

"Good idea." He helped her place the sheets on the sofa, tucking them in as if he made his own bed every day, something she highly doubted.

Finished, they both stood back, eying the couch as though it might come alive any second.

"What do we do now?" she asked.

He glanced around the room. "Want to play a game?"

"What kind of game?" She cocked her head and examined him through narrowed eyes.

His laugh reverberated through the room. "Board games. They've got the most popular ones. I noticed the boxes in the cupboard against the far wall when I was cleaning."

Since she spoke four languages but lacked any kind of sports knowledge, she figured she should stick with word games over trivia. "Is Scrabble there?" she asked.

A wry smile twisted his lips and revealed that irresistible dimple. "How did I know you were going to say that? Only common English words count," he called over his shoulder as he pulled the box from the ornately carved sideboard.

She folded herself onto one end of the sofa as Caleb set up the game between them, providing a few feet of breathing—or in her case, thinking—space. "How long have you been back in Thailand?" he asked as he put his first word on the board. *Rappel.*

"Three months." She added the word *pretty*, using one of his *p*'s.

"I'm surprised you moved back during monsoon season if it's so hard for you."

"I had originally planned to wait. But my grandfather broke his leg, and then Grandma came down with pneumonia. So I returned early to help them." *And to escape the pitying looks I received as I sat alone watching* Love Island *while my ex was undoubtedly out having fun with his new traffic-warden girlfriend.* Even monsoon season had seemed preferable to staying in London.

He added the word *rock* to the board. "Will you go back to the UK once your grandparents have recovered?"

"No." She placed an *a* and *r* in front of the *c* from his word *rock*. "Since the moment I left Thai soil, I've wanted to return."

"You're living the dream, then?"

She heaved a sigh and watched him turn her *arc* into *arcade*. She should have known she couldn't beat this man at anything.

"It's not quite like I imagined it," she admitted.

"I know that feeling. I always thought that if I started my own company, I'd be in control and able to do whatever I wanted."

She placed the word *apple* on the board. "Can't you?"

"No. I now have commitments to shareholders and clients, contracts to read, and meetings to chair or attend—all the things I never wanted."

"So why do it, then? Why not put someone else in charge?"

It was his turn to sigh. "Because I'm too competitive. I have to be the best. And I have to keep busy."

"Being stranded here must be hell for you, then." She stared at her letter tiles, but only half her brain was able to focus on the game. The rest was consumed by the man across from her. Every time he leaned forward to place another word on the board, his T-shirt would stretch tight across his shoulders.

"Actually, it's not too bad. I'm kind of enjoying the change of pace."

This pace was her new life. He'd soon grow bored with it. She ruthlessly stamped out the niggle of disappointment before it could morph into discontent. They both added a few additional small words to the game.

"What's the difference between your dream and reality?" he asked.

She stared at her tiles, but the only word she could see was *fail*. With his comments about challenging himself and being the best, the word probably wasn't even in his vocabulary. "I thought that being home, I'd finally fit in."

"And you don't?" He formed the word *chalk* on the board and speared her with his sharp green eyes.

"I don't fit in anywhere. I'm too Western to be Thai and too Thai to be Western." Her guts twisted at the confession. Her soul was homeless.

"London's quite a cosmopolitan city. I'm surprised you don't feel you belong there. A young, beautiful woman such as yourself, I'd imagine the world would be yours for the taking."

She wasn't quite sure what to make of his compliment. "My views of London are probably tainted by my early days there. I didn't speak English, I didn't dress like everyone else, and I was shocked at everything. School was very rough the first few years."

"I'm sorry to hear that. Did it get better?" His eyes flashed with sympathy before dropping to the letter tiles in front of him.

"Eventually. I started to act like everyone else. I practiced speaking English until I could do so without a Thai accent. I dressed like the rest of the girls and got over my naïveté. But I still felt like a fraud. I conformed to be accepted. But I was never happy."

He nodded. Although what a powerful billionaire could know about feeling left out, she had no idea. He waited while she fiddled with her tiles, but all she managed was to add an *s* to one of his words.

"What are you going to do?" he asked. "Stay in Thailand but live in one of the larger cities?"

"I don't like city life. I guess I'll just stay here. I'm sure the feeling will pass, and eventually it will be like I'd never been away."

A loud crack of thunder shook the room again. Caleb's hand reached out and took hers, squeezing it lightly. "You okay?"

Her eyes met his, and she waited for the panic to overtake her. Her heart rate sped up and a clamminess came over her skin, but the sheer terror she'd come to expect never materialized. She forced her mind to concentrate on the warmth of Caleb's hand and took a deep breath. "I'm fine." As soon as the words were out of her mouth, she regretted them. It was probably her last chance to be held in his arms, and she'd blown it.

His eyes held hers for a moment longer before dropping to the board. "All I've got left are vowels. I'll concede this game if you'll agree to a rematch."

He was obviously trying to distract her, so she nodded and handed over her remaining letter tiles. To do so, she had to remove her hand from his, and she instantly missed the comfort. He cleared the board. Clenching her teeth together, she picked seven more from the bag and concentrated on her new letters.

The storm wasn't nearly as fierce as the others, and soon she was able to relax. Caleb teased her about some of the lame words she put down, saying that for a woman who spoke four languages, she should be able to come up with something more original than *cat*. His words were mostly about dangerous sports. After the third round of Scrabble, she got up to stretch. Wandering over to the open window, she stared out at the dark, ominous sky.

"I don't think the rain is going to stop today," she said.

"I'd come to the same conclusion," Caleb replied from right behind her. His warm breath tickled down her back. Awareness of him swept through her like a tsunami. "We might as well make ourselves comfortable, since it looks like we're here for another night. And before you say anything, you're sleeping with me again."

She swallowed. If she believed in fate, it would be telling her to have an affair with Caleb. But she was the master of her own destiny, if not her body.

They switched out Scrabble for Monopoly, which Caleb soundly trounced her at. When her stomach started to grumble, she cooked dinner while he kept her entertained with amusing stories of disastrous camping trips. If he noticed the sharp note to her laughter or the rigidity of her spine, he said nothing.

Being stuck inside and trying to keep her lusty thoughts in control, especially about sleeping with him again, had her on edge. As eight thirty rolled around and Caleb yawned for the third time, she was ready for the inevitable.

When she entered his room after changing once more into his T-shirt, he was already under the sheets, a white undershirt covering his upper half. She bit back a groan of disappointment. As soon as she slid under the covers, he turned his back to her, and based on his regular breathing, he fell asleep in seconds. At some point in the night, though, he turned over, because she woke to find him spooning her, his hand splayed possessively over her stomach.

Sharing a bed with him: it was so wrong that it felt so right.

**

The next morning dawned bright and clear, and both Caleb and his suitcase were gone when Malee woke. Had he left already, desperate to get away from the needy woman who couldn't even sleep alone. Her throat tightened, and it was hard to draw in a deep breath.

She changed once more into her shorts and T-shirt and packed up her things. Caleb stood on the front lawn, staring at the view. His hair was damp, and his blue shirt clung to his body, his powerful thighs encased in light brown trousers.

"We should head down the road before we get caught in another storm," he said by way of greeting.

"Yes, of course."

The morning sun had dried up the mud, so she managed to get into the vehicle without face-planting again. Caleb drove carefully down the mountain. There was even more debris on the road from yesterday's storms. When they got near where the road had been washed away, he parked and they both got out.

A larger chunk of the mountainside had disappeared into the valley. The previous five-meter gap was now at least fifteen meters wide. But parked on the village side was her cousin's Jeep, surrounded by a dozen men.

And her grandmother was there, dressed in her tribal costume of black jacket, fluffy red scarf, loose but elaborately striped trousers, and embroidered black turban, complete with silver tassels dangling around her temples. Oh God, what was Yai up to now?

"Malee, are you both okay?" Bodin called out in Thai.

"Yes, we're fine," she answered.

"Have you slept with him yet?" her grandmother asked in Mien.

Malee's cheeks flamed while she searched the faces of the other villagers, but no one appeared to have understood the outrageous question. She was probably the only grandchild who had bothered to learn her grandparents' native languages, having lived with them for four years following her father's death before she'd joined her mother in England.

"Grandmother, what a question to ask!" There, she'd neatly avoided that discussion. Because technically they *had* slept together, just not in the way her gran meant.

"It's a perfectly logical question, girl. Look at him!

Siliwan in the grocery store said he's the best-looking man she's ever seen. And I agree. Apart from your grandfather, that is. But my tastes have always leaned toward darker meat."

She would have wished for the ground to swallow her alive, but since that was still a distinct possibility, she took another step back from the edge.

"Grandma, he's my boss. We didn't get stranded to have an affair."

"Maybe the spirits have willed it. It's time you married, girl. And this one looks to be a fine specimen."

"He's a foreigner. I want to stay in Thailand."

Her grandmother's eyes darted once more to Caleb. "Do you? Don't turn your back on adventure because you're scared. None of you would be here now if I hadn't left my people and followed my heart."

"This has nothing to do with my heart. And everything to do with being trapped by a landslide."

"Bah. Take a chance, Malee-ya. Just don't get pregnant unless he's willing to marry you. Because these Thai"—she gestured at Bodin and his entourage—"are very conservative. What is his date of birth? I need to make sure you are compatible." Her gran had to come from the one tribe in the area in which pre-marital sex was not a taboo and compatibility was based on an astrological calendar. "Just to be safe, though, I will perform an engagement ceremony."

Dear God, please, no! But her grandmother's gods weren't Malee's, so they didn't pay any attention to her plea. Her grandmother hopped around on one foot while chanting nonsense, waved some feathers above her head, and then spat into a handful of uncooked rice before flinging the grains into the ravine between them. Not for the first time, Malee wondered if her gran had left her people willingly or if she'd been exiled for offending the spirits. At least the villagers looked amused. Caleb too, when she dared to glance in his direction.

"Okay, Gran, we're good now," Malee yelled as her elder started singing about fertility.

Bodin gave Yai an exasperated look before, for once in his life, rescuing Malee from more embarrassment. "What does he think of the place? Have you convinced him to buy it yet?"

"It's hard to get a guy to love a place when he's stuck there against his will."

"Try harder. It's important, Malee. For the … village."

Forget that she'd been stranded with a complete stranger, a foreign man, for the past forty-eight hours. Just remember the village needed her to do the impossible. She forced her temper back down, her relief at his interruption already gone. "Can you rescue us?"

"We've been here for twenty minutes, and the only way for you to cross is if we tie a rope to both vehicles and you make your way over on that. The ground it too unstable to attempt anything else." Bodin held up a thin rope for her to see. From where she stood, it resembled dental floss.

"Who are all these people? What's everyone saying?" Caleb, who seemed to have been doing his own slope assessment, now stood at her side. From across the divide, Yai grinned from ear to ear.

"The woman is my grandmother." *In case you don't recognize her with clothes on.* "The man in front is my cousin. He has a long Thai name, but we call him Bodin. And the others are just locals, here to see if they can help." *Or watch Gran.*

"Can they?"

"They're suggesting we cross by rope tied to both vehicles." Even saying the words out loud, her heart nearly leapt from her chest. The distance was too far, the drop too steep. There was no way she'd make it without falling. She wrapped her arms around herself and waited for Caleb's reply.

"Can you manage it?" he asked.

She shook her head, her throat so clogged with fear, she could barely breathe. "I'm not so good with heights." Or with plummeting to her death.

"Tell them to throw over the rope," Caleb said.

She searched his face. Was he going to force her to go across? Or leave her on her own?

Chapter Six

Caleb did a quick assessment of the situation. Years of rock climbing and his knowledge of terrain confirmed the villagers' assessment. There was no way across except by rope. Malee's eyes were huge, her knuckles white where she clenched her hands into fists.

They'd have to stay a few more days and find another way out. The line landed near his feet and when he bent to pick it up, a little sob broke from Malee. He wanted to wrap his arms around her, tell her everything would be okay, but he wasn't sure how that would go down with the men across the ravine. From the huge smile on her grandmother's face, though, she didn't seem to mind her granddaughter being stranded with a strange man. He only wished he'd understood what she and Malee had been saying.

"We'll wait on this side for a proper rescue. Do you have a pen and paper?" he asked. She walked to the SUV and returned a moment later with a notepad and pen. "Do any of them speak English?" He tilted his head toward the villagers across the divide.

Malee called out to them, and after a few answered, she turned back to him. "No. Why?"

Damn. He was totally reliant on her ability to get his message relayed correctly, or they'd be stuck for weeks. "I need someone to contact my office in Canada and get a helicopter to airlift us out of here. Ask one of them to find an English speaker to pass the message on to my colleague."

She called over and had a conversation with one of the men. "His sister works at a tourist hotel in Chiang Rai. He'll take your note there today and get someone to call your office."

He put the paper, a rock for weight, and a few bills to cover the international phone call into a plastic bag he found in the glove box. He secured the bag to the rope and threw it back over to the other side.

"They're going to send some food over," Malee said as the line once again landed near his feet. "We just have to hold onto our end."

One of the other men climbed onto the hood of the Jeep, attached a set of wheels with hooks onto the rope, and soon several bags of food were whizzing their way over to their side. Malee had a quick look at the provisions and seemed satisfied.

"Got everything you need?" he asked.

"Enough that we won't starve. They're suggesting we meet back here the day after tomorrow, and they'll update us on the rescue efforts."

"Sounds good."

Malee said a few more things to her cousin in Thai, while Caleb put the bags of food in the back of the SUV. He spied some canned meat, fruit and vegetables, rice and noodles. Considering Malee'd made a delicious meal out of rice and canned tuna yesterday, his mouth watered at the thought of what she'd be able to create with this bounty.

When he returned to the front of the vehicle, Malee was staring at her feet, nodding at whatever the man across from her was saying. Her hands were again clenched into fists at her side. By the time the exchange finished, she vibrated with anger.

"What was that about?"

"Just my cousin being his normal idiot self. He thinks he can tell me what to do and how to do it."

Caleb glanced back at the man Malee had been talking with. His arms were crossed over his chest, his feet apart as though ready for a fight. If they hadn't been separated by a fifteen-meter gap, Caleb had a feeling the man would be toe-to-toe with him. "Does he think I'll take advantage of you?"

Malee quickly looked up but didn't quite meet his gaze. Her eyes shot to her grandmother, who had retreated to the vehicle on the other side, seeming a bit winded after her … performance. "No. Nothing like that."

"But your grandmother does? Is that what all that singing and dancing was about? My, uh, bits aren't going to fall off, are they?" The pink on her cheeks darkened, and a strained laugh escaped Malee's lips.

"No. I told you, my grandmother is eccentric, and she enjoys making a spectacle of herself." She walked around to the passenger side of the SUV and got in. "Bodin was just being a self-centered jerk."

Before he started the vehicle, he glanced over at her. She had her hands folded primly in her lap and her bottom lip between her teeth. "Why didn't you tell him to mind his own business?"

"Because he's family and my elder. Respect is the cornerstone of Thai culture. Even if he's wrong, I can't say so, at least not in public."

"So he can just stand there and berate you with half the village listening."

"Something like that."

Was there more to what her cousin had said? And her grandmother? There had clearly been some sort of message passed there. He ran a hand through his hair. He hadn't stopped to consider how being stranded with him could damage Malee's reputation and impact her future.

He cleared his throat. "Is this going to be a problem? I don't want to make things difficult for you." Although what exactly they could do to fix the issue, he didn't know. She refused to cross with the rope, and he couldn't leave her at the hotel by herself. What if there was another storm? The thought brought back the memory of her warm body pressed against his in the night, her exotic scent enveloping him... He forced his mind to the issue at hand before it dared wander to yesterday morning's bathing scene.

"No. Don't worry. You're not going to be forced to marry me. And there are no interesting men in this village anyway, so it's not like I'm ruining my chances."

"Malee—"

"Can we just drop the subject, please? You're my boss. I'm not about to sleep with you—okay, I did sleep with you but—I mean, we're not going to have sex or anything. Are we?"

Was the note of hopefulness in her voice just his imagination?

"First, until we're rescued, I'm not your boss, just a friend. Don't worry, you'll still get paid, but I don't want your Thai sensibilities to get in the way of what you want. You won't offend me or make me think less of you for standing up for yourself. Second, anything that happens or doesn't happen is strictly between us. I will never, ever coerce or force you into anything. And no one else need ever know. What happens at Destiny Resort stays at Destiny Resort."

She looked at him then, a hint of a smile on her face. "Is that what you're thinking of calling this place—Destiny Resort? That's a horrible name."

He started the car and headed back up the hill. "You think so? Because I'm thinking the only people who will want to stay here, if it ever reopens, would be those interested in alternative lifestyles. Most people expect electricity and running water in their accommodations."

"It has electricity and running water, once the generators are going. Besides, people who follow alternative lifestyles rarely have the money to pay what you'd have to charge to make this place work. What about stressed-out executives who need to completely detox from work? There's no Wi-Fi, no computers, no mobile phone reception. There could be a satellite phone for emergencies, but aside from that, they'd be completely cut off and have to reconnect with their significant other … or with themselves."

How many cliffs had he climbed to escape the demands of his business and have a little 'me' time? "Interesting idea. I'll give it some thought." Because he had little else to occupy his brain for the next two days.

Aside from resisting his desire for Malee.

This time, when he parked by the hotel, he made sure to avoid any mud puddles. "Since we'll be here for a little longer, I'll see if I can get the generators running. But the diesel fuel has probably gone bad." He didn't want to get her hopes up that they'd have lights tonight.

"After I make breakfast, I'll do what I can to make the inside a little more comfortable," she said.

All he needed to be comfortable was Malee in his bed, but that was about as likely to happen as the lights coming on.

Unless destiny had a better plan.

***

Malee stood in the doorway and admired her handiwork. The room looked good. She'd wiped down every surface and taken the curtains outside and beat the dust out of them, pretending they were Bodin. If he inferred one more time that if the hotel sale fell through, it would be her fault…

Caleb had been fiddling with the generators all morning. When she'd passed the little hut on her way to get more water from the stream, a string of curses had turned the air blue. It would be nice to have electricity, but with the gas-powered lights and Caleb's presence, the dark didn't seem so ominous any more.

Her stomach rumbled, reminding her she should probably make a start on lunch.

"The room looks good," Caleb said from right behind her. She whirled around, almost spilling the dirty water from the bucket she held.

He took the pail from her hand.

"Sorry, I lost track of time. I'll make lunch now."

"You're not here to serve me, Malee. *We'll* make lunch."

She tipped her head to one side, not quite sure what to make of him. He was unlike any other man she'd met—sweet, gentle, caring—but she had a feeling he'd be a fierce protector and a devil in the boardroom. So far, though, he'd taken mostly an observer's role in the kitchen. "What are your cooking skills like?"

"I've been known to grill a mean steak."

"Unfortunately, steak is not on the menu. But if you promise not to hack off a finger, I'll let you chop the vegetables."

He laughed and followed her from the room. "I think I may have gotten the generator working. But there's not a lot of good diesel left, so we'll have to ration our use of it. Especially if we're here longer than two days."

"Oh my God, I could so kiss you right now," she said without thinking.

"All right, then." He put down the bucket of water he'd been carrying and puckered his lips.

It was probably the stupidest thing she'd done in a long time. But what had being sensible gotten her? A lonely heart and no prospects. She went up on her tiptoes and put a hand on Caleb's chest for balance. His heart beat strong and steady beneath her palm, unlike her own, which raced as though she were about to kiss the hottest man she'd ever met.

It was just a kiss, for goodness' sake. When her lips

met his, however, the idea that it was just a kiss went out the window. Her tongue traced the outline of Caleb's lower lip before she pulled it into her mouth, sucking it in and out to match the rhythm her hips had taken up. She was about to move away while she still could when Caleb's arm came around her waist and held her closer to his body.

He allowed her another minute to lead the kiss before he took over. Alternating between plundering her mouth and seducing her lips, he led her into a world of pleasure. She pressed her body closer to his, rubbing her breasts against his chest, wishing she hadn't put her bra on today. Caleb's groan filled the air.

His hands moved to her hips, but rather than lift her up so she straddled his waist, he set her away from him. Both their chests heaved as they drew in ragged breaths.

He ran a hand through his hair. Was it her imagination, or was it shaking slightly? "If we don't stop now, I'll carry you to bed and we'll spend the rest of the afternoon and probably most of the evening testing the springs on the mattress upstairs."

That sounded good to her. But he'd stopped, so he obviously thought it a bad idea. And no matter what he said, she was still an employee and needed to conduct herself professionally if she hoped to get a good reference from him.

She focused on the floor at her feet. "I'll start lunch. Can you bring more water up? There's a bucket by the back door."

He nodded, as though relieved for the chance to get away from her. When he left to get the water, she slumped against the wall. *Holy doodle*, no kiss had ever made her melt before. She prayed there wouldn't be another storm tonight, because she didn't think she'd be able to sleep in his bed without spontaneously igniting.

She straightened her hair and hurried to the kitchen. Keeping her focus on making the resort as appealing as possible had to be her priority. If she could convince him to invest in the place, her mother could come home and Malee could get work, and so could many others from the village. And Bodin … well, he could still take a flying leap from the nearest cliff, but at least he'd be forced to acknowledge that she had accomplished the impossible. Surely that was worth forfeiting some personal pleasure. Her tongue ran over her lips. The village had better appreciate her sacrifice. Too bad she'd never be able to tell them.

She managed to prep most of lunch before Caleb returned, not surprised that he'd obviously taken the opportunity to wash, or cool down.

"Can you set the table out on the terrace again?" She wanted him to appreciate the view, see the potential in the place. It was time for operation *This Is Your Destiny*.

She brought out the plates, which were heaped with a version of pad thai her mother had taught her to make when provisions were low, as they had been many times in her life. Not having the luxuries other kids took for granted had never bothered her. But it was upsetting to see her mum work two jobs, rarely sleep, and worry about everything. If Malee could reunite the family so they could all support each other … maybe then she'd feel settled.

"I never get tired of the view," she said.

"It is rather spectacular. I imagine it with mist in the valleys, exotic birds calling to each other, a sense of mystery, of excitement in the air..."

She let him dwell on that for a moment. "It is like that many mornings. You could take a photo of that and put in on the front page of the brochure or website, with the heading *Renew, Relax, Rejoice*."

He turned from the view to search her face, his eyes lingering a long moment on her lips. Was he remembering the kiss as well? Heat flooded her core. "Sounds like you've put some thought into this. Tell me, Malee, what is your vision for this place?"

She was supposed to keep her mouth shut. After all, she'd only been hired as his translator. But with her family's future at stake, she couldn't pretend indifference.

"As I mentioned before, it would make an amazing retreat for stressed-out executives. Something less dangerous than hanging off a cliff. Of course, you'd have to upgrade a lot of things. All the rooms would have to be executive suites, and probably the maximum you'd be able to accommodate would be ten couples at a time. But that would add to its exclusivity. In fact, you could probably get corporations to send their top execs here to avoid burnout."

Rather than laugh at her excitement, he put down his fork and leaned closer. "What kind of amenities would this stressed-exec retreat have?"

"The usual, I expect." The most luxurious resort she'd ever seen was in Chiang Mai where her dad had worked, only that one had catered for families. "Massages and maybe some counseling or yoga classes to help them relax … top-notch food, a few guided hikes in the rain forest … and elephants. Everyone loves elephants."

"Interesting. However, I already foresee three problems with your idea."

Her heart sank, but at least he hadn't dismissed her suggestions completely. "What problems?"

"First and most important would be access and egress. I can hardly have top executives come here when they don't know if they'll be able to leave."

"That's easy to fix. As I told you, there's a helipad at the top of that mountain." She pointed to the peak behind the resort. "It may need a little maintenance, but it should be fine. It's always been a bare spot for some reason. My grandma's people have a story about a woman weeping over a man from another tribe who betrayed her. Evidently she shed toxic tears and poisoned the ground so nothing grew."

"What a great story. It adds a bit of romance to the resort."

"If you consider a broken heart romantic. According to the legend, she killed herself afterward."

"Hmm. Maybe we'd better leave that part out."

Was he seriously considering her proposal? Or only humoring her? After all, being stranded with a weepy woman wasn't something most men would sign up for. "What's your second problem?"

"Staffing. How can we get a top chef, massage people, therapists, and so on to live in the middle of nowhere? And if most of the accommodation is taken by staff, that will further reduce the number of rooms we have available for guests. I just don't think it's economically viable."

"Hire locals. They can live in the village and commute. You could keep a skeleton staff on hand in case of road closures, but this is the first slide I've ever heard of, so it's not like it happens every day. We can probably forge a path across the mountain so many could walk or ride motorbikes in."

He gave her the patient smile of a kindergarten teacher trying to explain to a student that they had to share the crayons. "As much as I'd love to support the local workforce, the level of service required for the type of establishment you've outlined would have to be world-class. I'm not sure there's that type of talent available locally."

"My mother is sous-chef at the Thai restaurant in the Lancaster Hotel in London. She wants to come home to Thailand to be with her parents. Currently, she's the only one of us with a regular income so she has to stay in the UK. But if she had a job here…"

"Your mother wants to leave a top chef position in a world-renowned city to come back here?"

The incredulity in his voice said it all. He might like the place, but he could never see himself staying here for any length of time. The thought was the huge stop sign she needed to quit fantasizing about the man. He had the potential to ruin her for a nice, normal guy.

"She's tired of working sixteen-hour days and being so far from home."

He nodded, although his eyes didn't light with

understanding. Maybe he had no affinity with his home or family.

"Okay, so there may be a world-class chef willing to relocate, but what about other staff? You suggested a counselor and massage therapists."

"I'm sure we could find people to fill those positions. In fact, I have someone in mind for a counselor." The woman who had helped her deal with her father's tragic passing now lived locally.

"And the elephants? I have to tell you that Westerners are told not to go on elephant rides because the animals are cruelly treated when they're trained."

Malee sighed. "I know. And now there are many unemployed elephants who are starving because their mahouts can't afford to feed them. Maybe we could find something else for them to do, like massages. How cool would that be? Massage by elephant trunk."

"I'm not sure I'd be willing to trust an elephant's trunk anywhere near my junk."

She laughed. "Okay, that might be too much. But you could keep a couple around just for the aesthetic. Kind of like a hotel mascot."

He simply nodded, but the skepticism she'd seen on his face earlier had lessened somewhat. "Interesting ideas, but that brings us to the biggest hurdle in turning this resort around."

"What's that?"

"The cost. I can't honestly recommend that my brother buy this property for even a quarter of the price asked. The money's he's put down to secure his bid is more than it's worth."

"But if you could make a deal with the sellers…"

"Even then, the capital needed to turn this place around isn't in my brother's budget. He wanted this property to save his company, not take it down once and for all."

She swallowed down her disappointment. "What about you?"

"Me?" He'd picked up his fork to finish his lunch but put it down again as she reached over and put her hand on top of his.

"You could invest in it."

He was shaking his head before she even finished her sentence. "I got out of the hotel business years ago. And for good reason. No way in hell am I getting back in that game."

She sighed and turned her attention to her food, swallowing her disappointment.

Too bad this wasn't a game to her…

Chapter Seven

Caleb leaned a hip against the stainless-steel counter in the kitchen as Malee meticulously wiped down all the food prep surfaces. Her cooking skills were first class. With a little more training, she could be the chef here. If there was a *here* to chef. He'd meant every word he'd said; the cards were stacked against reopening the resort. So why did he still want to find a way to do it? Hotels were his brother's business. But the disappointment in Malee's eyes when he'd told her he wasn't interested in investing his own money had given him a queasy sensation in the pit of his stomach.

"What shall we do for the rest of the afternoon?" He hung up the towel he'd used for the dishes, spreading it out to dry. Although how anything dried in this humidity, he had no idea. He'd already taken two ice-cold showers in the waterfall today, and still his T-shirt clung to his skin.

Malee glanced up. She'd already scrubbed that area of the counter twice. "I thought I'd clean a few more rooms."

"Why bother? It's only us here. Why don't we explore the area?"

She cocked her head as if considering her options, then a smile lit her face like the sun appearing after weeks of rain. His breath caught in his throat. He forced his gaze from her lips and the sudden urge to taste them again. After the first kiss, he knew she was an addiction he couldn't handle. And it wasn't fair to lead her on when he had absolutely no intention of taking things farther than his bed. Malee did not come across as a woman who indulged in casual affairs. When his mind flashed to her five years from now, she had a gold band on her left ring finger, one child on the hip, and another holding onto her skirt. The queasiness in his stomach became a full roil.

Just because he was terrified of commitment, of being responsible for someone else's happiness, didn't mean that others shouldn't indulge in permanent relationships. He'd realized early in his adulthood that after a few weeks with the same woman, he grew restless and felt the need to move on to another challenge. So his irritation at the idea of Malee with another man was beyond ridiculous.

"All right. But don't blame me if you fall in love with the place." She rinsed out her cloth and hung it to dry next to his dishtowel.

"My heart is pretty love-proof, but do your best." Had he said that to remind himself, or to warn her?

Her gaze stroked his body, leaving invisible scorch marks on his skin. "Do you have better shoes? Not the nice leather ones you had on yesterday?"

"I brought a pair of hikers, but what about you?" She had on the ragged sandals she'd worn to the airport. The only other shoes she had with her were the heels she'd put on for dinner. "Maybe we'd better put off exploring."

"Nah, I'm a local. These are good enough. Or bare

feet when it gets slippery."

He'd take her word for it, and if he had to carry her at some point, that would be a bonus. "Okay, give me a sec to change."

When he met her on the back steps ten minutes later, Malee had wound her hair up in a knot at the top of her head, leaving the long, delicate column of her neck bare for his lips to explore. *Damn.* That wasn't the type of escapade he'd intended.

Although...

No, he had to keep his hands off. Then he noticed the large machete she held at her side. *Right.* If he wanted to keep all his limbs attached, he'd better add his lips to the parts he needed to keep in check.

"Ready?" Her gaze locked with his, and the air between them sizzled. A smart man would stay at the resort, find a comfy chair, and read through the dozens of reports he'd brought with him. But he'd never been one to turn down an adventure.

"Ready. Where should we head first?"

"I thought we'd go up to the helipad. It has a great view. Then down the other side of the mountain. If I remember correctly, there's another waterfall and pool and maybe a cave. It's been years since I've wandered around here."

He scanned the sky. So far, all clear. But yesterday's storm had seemed to come out of nowhere. "We probably shouldn't go too far in case the weather turns again."

Her soft smile didn't even waver. "I guess we'll just have to see what destiny has in store for us."

She set off to the left of the generator building and whether through knowledge, instinct, or luck, found a path that led up the mountain. Although path might have been too grand a name for the tiny track that had only slightly less dense vegetation than the surrounding hillside. Malee hacked at some of the more stubborn branches and fronds that blocked their path.

"I can do that." He tried to take the big knife from her hand, but she held fast.

"I'm good. It's therapeutic."

Before he could ask what was wrong, she turned back to hacking at the flora. Was she releasing her frustration over her cousin's comments? Or was something else bothering her? After about twenty minutes, they came to a clearing. The tribal woman's tears must have been incredibly toxic to prevent the jungle from taking over here as well.

Speaking of indigenous dramas... "Was your grandmother concerned about you being stranded here with me?"

He couldn't tell if Malee was blushing or not because her face was flushed with the heat and exercise. "Um, not so much concerned as ... sensing an opportunity. She wants to see me settled with my own husband."

He stopped walking. "That ceremony she performed... We're not married, are we?"

"No, of course not. As I said, she's eccentric. She just makes stuff up to get a reaction." But her eyes darted away and there was a definite nervous quality to her answer.

He hadn't signed anything, so he was probably still

single. He should be relieved, shouldn't he? "I admit, I didn't know there were non-Thai people in this area."

"Yes, there are like seven or eight main tribes in northern Thailand, and most of those have several branches. My gran's tribe, the Mien, are also called the Yao. They originated in China and their writing uses Chinese characters. There are around thirty thousand of them in Thailand and quite a few in Laos, some even in the United States." She took a drink of water, then carried on climbing the hill.

"That's it?" he asked. "I get a twenty-minute lecture on water buffalo but barely thirty seconds on a quarter of your heritage?"

That got a little laugh. "To understand the Mien, or any of the tribes really, you have to spend time with them. One thing that is important with my gran's people is helping neighbors. In fact, that's how she got sick. She was nursing her friend who had a bad cold. Yai is a bit crazy, but I wouldn't have her any other way. She's unique, and I love her."

And he could tell that Malee was loved back. He'd never been close to any of his family. Would it have made a difference in his life if he had?

The last hundred meters to the top were as strenuous as the rest with the hot Thai sun beating down on them. His shirt was soaked with sweat and his shorts were stuck in places they shouldn't be.

At the summit, however, his discomfort was forgotten as he took in the view. Mountains and valleys stretched out before him like a lumpy green quilt. Rice terraces dotted several slopes, and a lazy river wound its way past small villages with the houses all raised on stilts. Perched on the side of a rock-faced mountain in the distance were white-domed temples, appearing as though they'd been dropped there by a careless god.

Hauling in a deep breath, tension seemed to pour from him along with the sweat. And despite the liquid loss, he felt as if he were an inch taller. The knots in his neck, which he'd long assumed were permanent, eased.

"Magical, isn't it? Imagine if this was the first thing you'd seen when you arrived." Malee's quiet voice flowed through him like the river through the valley.

"It is beautiful." He snapped a couple of photos. His phone battery had died the previous night, but his housekeeper had slipped the old Canon into his bag when she'd packed for him.

After taking in the scenery, he checked out the area. The top of the hill was perfectly level, as though it had been shaved down or sliced off. Provided the weather was decent, it would be easy for a helicopter to land. But it was still a dangerous, half-hour hike down to the resort. How would any desk-bound executive be able to do it without having a heart attack? Liability insurance would cost a fortune. But after seeing the light back in Malee's eyes, he decided not to mention it to her.

"Of course, if you take on the resort, we'll have to install some kind of gondola system to get guests and their luggage up and down the mountain."

She wasn't giving up on this. "Those cost millions, Malee."

"We'll see," she said.

The woman was tenacious, he'd give her that. What

would she be like as a lover? Their kiss in the hallway had been a revelation. He'd expected a shy peck on his cheek, not an all-out assault on his mouth. The midday sun had nothing on the heat of their embrace.

He wandered around the site, curious as to why the jungle hadn't claimed this bit of land. Without a geological survey, however, it would have to remain a mystery. Besides, the tribal legend was a better story.

While he explored, Malee peered into the jungle at the north end of the clearing. "I think this is the way," she called out.

Before he could respond, she'd disappeared, and only the *thwack* of her machete slicing through the foliage gave a clue to her whereabouts.

"Malee, wait up," he called, sliding down the slight path she'd made. The fallen vegetation made getting a secure foothold even more precarious. He'd likely fall on his ass, slide down, and take her with him. Good thing it wasn't raining. The scene from *Romancing the Stone*, where Michael Douglas and Kathleen Turner slide down the side of the mountain, flashed through his mind. At least no one was shooting at them.

Finally, he caught sight of her lithe body as she swayed side to side, slicing the jungle as she went. Perspiration dripped down the back of her neck and her T-shirt clung to her skin, outlining the lace of her bra. A soft sheen of moisture glistened on her bare legs. He probably wore the same expression on his face that Michael Douglas had in the movie: pure lust.

"If your arm is getting tired, I can take point for a while," he said. His offer was less chivalry and more an attempt to preserve his sanity. Following behind her filled his head with too many erotic thoughts.

"I'm okay." Two more thwacks, and large leaves fell in her wake. "I think we're almost…" Three more swipes of the large knife. "…there." Malee scooted to her right as the jungle ended abruptly, giving him space on the tiny ledge overlooking a massive waterfall. The drop was three times that of the one near the hotel, and the pool at the bottom was twice as big. The water, a deep emerald green, looked so refreshing that he groaned.

Surprisingly, leading away from the tiny ledge on which they stood, a set of steps carved into the rock face led down to the pool.

Even better, next to the falling water was a perfect cliff face to climb. He might have to resist the temptation of Malee's body, but this was one passion he could indulge.

He slipped off his hiking boots and pulled out his climbing shoes, glad he'd had the foresight to bring them.

"You may just have sold me on the place," he said. He left his camera and pack beside a stunned Malee and scooted to the very edge of the ledge before leaping onto the cliff face.

Malee's cry of alarm was quickly drowned out by the thundering water less than a meter away from him. The rock was slippery with the spray off the falls, and he slid down several meters before he got a firm hold.

***

Malee bit down on her knuckles, her stomach heaving as Caleb slowly scaled the rock face next to the waterfall. The man was insane. A fall would surely kill him. Why would he risk his life for a few minutes of fun?

He'd been in the same spot now for a few minutes. Was he realizing the stupidity of what he was doing? Or was he about to lose his grip? God, how would she explain what happened to his family or her agency? *Yeah, so I was trying to convince him to buy the resort when he tumbled fifteen meters to his death.* Good luck getting another job after that.

She needed to turn around so she didn't see him fall. But the play of his muscles was on full display now that he'd taken off his shirt, and the flex of his thighs and the bulge of his biceps as he heaved his divine body up another half meter were too compelling to miss. *Besides, I'll have to give a full report to the authorities when he killed himself.*

Damn the man. How could he be so sweet and gentle, helping her with her fears, and then act like such an arse the next minute? He was more like her father than she'd wanted to acknowledge. Despite her fledgling feelings for Caleb, and the way he made her body come alive with just a look, there was no chance they could have a relationship. She wouldn't live her life constantly worried that her husband would kill himself with his next reckless, thrill-seeking adventure.

She should never have brought him here. She'd wanted to show him the waterfall and the steps the previous resort owners had carved into the rocks, intending this to be a hiking destination for guests. How was she to know that Caleb would take one look at the waterfall and decide to climb the damn thing? And just how the hell did he think he was going to get back down? The pool here wasn't deep enough to dive into from that height.

Miraculously, he was near the top now. She needed to find a way up the hill to meet him. There had to be some means to get to the top of the waterfall from the hill behind them. While she was trying to figure out how they could meet up, Caleb began a careful descent. Her pulse still hadn't returned to normal, however, by the time he stood next to her once more.

A huge smile curved his lips, and her heart rate sped up again. She worked hard to keep the not-amused glare on her face under the radiance of his joy.

"You could have died," she said, glad her voice remained even.

"But I didn't. That was amazing, although if it had just rained, the part I climbed would have been under water, too." He glanced up at the small patch of sky visible. Nothing but blue. Having witnessed how fast storms could suddenly appear, he should have had more sense.

"Do you always do stupid stuff like that?"

The wattage of his smile dimmed and his gaze caressed her face. "Not always."

"Well, don't do it again when you're with me. What would I tell people if you fell?"

His eyes narrowed, and it might have been a trick of the light and her subsiding panic, but he appeared even larger in front of her. "I apologize if I scared you, but this is how I live my life. I won't change. For anyone."

"What if you were married and had a wife and children who depended on you?" Stupid as it seemed, since they had no chance at a permanent relationship, her breath halted, waiting for his answer.

A flicker of something flashed in his eyes before it disappeared. "I don't see that ever happening, so the question is irrelevant."

The breath whooshed out of her on a sigh. Her heart sank as whatever hope had been keeping it afloat flew off like air escaping from a balloon. She turned away so he couldn't see her disappointment and clue in that she'd been thinking about them together.

"There's a path back to the resort." She pointed at the carved steps, some in better shape than others. "I'm hoping it's traversable. Otherwise we'll have to go back the way we came."

"Let's give it a go," he said. His deep voice was so near her ear, a shiver slid down her skin.

He's reckless, remember. But the warning did little to cool her desire.

She moved toward the first step, careful in case it was slippery from the recent rains. Caleb's large, warm hand grasped her upper arm, his fingers brushing her breast in the process. Her nipples instantly pebbled, visible through her thin bra and sweat-soaked T-shirt.

Glancing up at him, his blue eyes were once more lit with that mix of humor and desire she'd come to expect.

"I'll go first. Me, people can live without. But if you fall, we're really done for," he said.

Her voice would have undoubtedly come out breathy,

so she merely nodded. They made it safely down to the first landing, level with the waterfall's pool. Oh God, how good would a swim be right now?

Caleb released her arm, and before she could say anything, began stripping off his shoes. When he reached for the fastening of his shorts, she nearly melted. He wasn't going to skinny dip, was he? She closed her eyes to send up a silent prayer and caught a glimpse of him jumping into the water in his black boxer briefs. In two strokes, he was in the middle of pool. Dipping his head under, he then surfaced, pushing his wet, blond hair out of his eyes.

"Come on, Malee. It's refreshing."

She eyed the water and Caleb. Then her shorts and T-shirt. Oh, what the hell. No one else was around to see. She slipped them off while Caleb swam toward the waterfall. Clad only in her white bra and panties, she quickly entered the pool. The cold water stung her skin, but after a few seconds, it felt blissful. Cocooned by the jungle, with all sound muffled by the crashing water, it was possible, if only for a moment, to believe they were the only two humans alive.

Caleb must have had a similar thought, because he said, "The world could have come to an end and we would never know."

"Does that upset you?" Did he miss civilization? Or was he coming to enjoy a more peaceful lifestyle?

"Not as much as it should. I'm enjoying this escape from reality."

Except *his* escape was *her* reality. Soon he'd be leaving, but she'd have to bear any consequences of their time together. Her grandmother may think that compatible birthdates were all that was required for a successful marriage, but Malee knew different. And she knew herself. She was vulnerable, desperate for love. And nothing good could come of falling for Caleb's charms. Except maybe a night she'd never forget.

He swam closer, droplets of water clinging to his powerful shoulders, and she had to fight the urge to lick them off. From the look in his eyes, he was fighting an urge to do something similar to her. The water was clear and she didn't dare look down, sure her white lingerie had become see-through, giving him a full view of her breasts.

"We should head back to the hotel," she said. Hypnotized by his eyes, she didn't move. Didn't want to move. Her protest was a token one, like the first polite rejection of a cup of tea even through you wanted one.

"Before we go, will you help me check an item off my bucket list?" He moved another few centimeters closer. The heat from his body warmed the water between them, the movement causing tiny waves to lap against her chest.

"What's that?" At this point, she wasn't sure she could deny him anything, but she didn't want to appear too eager.

"I'd like to kiss a beautiful woman next to a waterfall."

"And you've never done that before?"

"Nope. You'd be my first."

She glanced over his shoulder. The water was falling with such force, and she had no idea how deep it was closer to the falls. What if they lost their footing and got caught under the pressure of the water? Her stomach clenched. But what a way to go.

Her heart was lodged in her throat, making speech impossible, so she just nodded her head. Caleb's arm snaked around her waist and brought her body flush against his as he backed toward the splash zone. She soon lost her footing, but it appeared he could touch bottom. Her legs wrapped around his thighs, bringing her center against his pelvis. Despite the ice-cold water, there was a discernible bulge in his boxers.

With the spray hitting his back and the water buffeting around them, he reached out a hand and caressed her cheek. Their gazes locked, and all the reasons why she should keep her distance disappeared. Being this close to him—it was her version of climbing a cliff face with her bare hands. Dangerous yet thrilling.

His mouth was soft at first, tentatively sipping along her lips, tasting and coaxing her to respond. As soon as she opened up, his tongue swept inside, and the ferocity of the water had nothing on the swirl of emotions his kiss evoked. Her legs tightened around his, bringing his erection into direct contact with her core. His hand slid down her cheek and onto her shoulder before lowering into the water to tease her nipple through the fabric of her bra. Instinctively, she pushed her breast further into his hand. A low moan filled the air, but if her life depended on it, she couldn't tell which one of them it came from.

Her fingers were threaded through the hair at his nape while her other hand clutched at his back. She'd like to blame the rocking of her hips on the water, but it was the rhythm of the ancients taking over. No man had ever brought her to the edge of orgasm so quickly.

The hooks on the back of her bra gave way and the garment floated to the surface of the water, freeing her breasts for Caleb's direct caress. The straps were annoying on her arms and she wanted nothing between her and Caleb, so she slid them off and let the bra float away. His lips left hers to trace a path of fire down her throat and her head fell back into the water. He shifted her higher on his body until her shoulders were well above the water, her breasts floating before his face. Through her lowered lashes, she watched as he took one rock-hard nipple into his mouth. This time she knew the shout of pleasure came from her.

The sound seemed to bring Caleb back to his senses, because he released her breast and unhooked her legs from his waist.

"Thank you," he said, his voice husky with desire. "I can definitely cross that off my list."

If they were going to use each other for list elimination, she was writing a whole new one as they returned to the edge of the pool and got dressed again.

She wondered how many of the items she would get to check off before they were rescued. Of more immediate concern, however, was the location of the one and only bra she had with her.

Chapter Eight

Caleb carefully picked his way over the rough terrain, keeping a tight grip on Malee's hand. It was a good thing he needed to keep his eyes trained on the uneven ground, because her braless breasts jiggling under her wet T-shirt were calling to him so loudly he could barely think. Or maybe that was the pounding of unfulfilled lust in his body.

Malee's shout of pleasure as he'd sucked her nipple by the waterfall had brought him back to his senses. He couldn't take her there, with no protection. He shouldn't take her anyway. She was from a different world, one where intimacy was accompanied by love and led to permanent relationships and babies and all the things that usually sent him running for the hills. But now that his hands had felt her curves and his lips and tongue had tasted her, he wasn't sure he'd be able to resist if she offered herself to him.

With the machete, he cut back more of the overgrown vegetation. Soon he recognized *their* waterfall, the one near the resort. How had he not noticed the stone steps set to the side before? Probably because his thoughts had always been on his companion.

Either the owners hadn't completed the path, or the last few treads had been eroded by the water. There was a three-meter gap between the rock they stood on and the base.

He let go of Malee's hand for the first time since they'd pulled their clothes on by the swimming hole. "I'll go down first and then help you." He tossed the machete into the soft grass bank where he'd placed his towel on previous occasions, then scooted onto his stomach, his legs dangling over the edge. He slid his body down until he held the edge of the rock with his fingertips. From here the drop was less than a meter. Once on solid ground, he stood back so he could look up at her. "Okay, turn around and lower yourself the way I did."

"Caleb…" Her tremulous voice cut into him.

"You're safe, Malee. I will never let you fall."

Without further protest, she disappeared from view for a second until her legs appeared above him. He slid his hands up her calves to her thighs so she knew he held her. Suddenly all her weight was on him and he lost his grip on her damp skin for a second until he found purchase again under her breasts. Her T-shirt had ridden up, leaving her back and stomach bare.

"I've got you," he said, his voice more strained than normal. This woman was a handful in more ways than one.

He lowered her feet to the ground, his hands still under the fullness of her breasts, her shirt bunched up so the bottom of the naked, lush flesh rested against his hands. With just a flick of his thumbs, he could be caressing her nipples. Bringing them straight back to where they'd left off in the water half an hour ago.

Instead, he pulled her shirt down as he released his

grip, although nothing could be done to disguise the hard pebbles jutting against the damp fabric. Would she understand if he sent her back to the hotel while he took an icy, boner-reducing swim?

"We made it," she said, her face alive with relief. The smile she gave him radiated into his heart.

He quirked a smile at her. "I'm hurt that you ever doubted me." She went to smack him on the chest, but he caught her hand and held it against him.

"This may be easy for you, but I prefer to keep my feet safely on the ground."

"Where's the fun in that?" he teased. But her eyes once again reflected the fear he'd seen when he'd returned from climbing the rock face. He hadn't meant to scare her. The challenge had called to him, and he'd answered without thinking how it would affect her. He wouldn't make that mistake again, at least not while she was near.

"Our ideas of fun seem to be wildly different."

He wasn't sure about that. Kissing her, touching her—they'd both enjoyed that. Before he could remind her of their mutual pleasure with a repeat performance, a distant rumble bounced around them. A shiver wracked Malee's body, and he drew her into his arms once more. This time, though, seduction wasn't on his mind. Okay, that was a bare-assed lie, but care and concern had at least relegated it to second place. She shifted her body against his. Seduction and care were now battling for first. "Let's get back to the hotel and make a start on dinner."

Hand in hand, they scrambled up the path and around

the back of the hotel, only to come to an abrupt halt. A huge elephant lay stretched out on the grass beside the kitchen garden. All the tall grass had been ripped up and consumed by the massive animal.

"Do you think it's friendly?" Malee asked.

"What happens if it's not?" Dealing with angry elephants wasn't on his résumé.

The pachyderm lifted its head and swished its tail at the sound of Caleb's voice. That was a good sign, wasn't it? As they took a few steps closer, the massive animal lumbered to its feet. Malee froze, and Caleb stepped between her and the elephant.

Another clap of thunder, closer this time, shattered the stillness of the air. The hairs on his arm stood up, and Malee's hands tightened on his waist. The elephant's trunk raised in the air, smelling them both, but he made no aggressive moves.

Caleb inched toward the hotel's back door, keeping himself between Malee and the giant animal.

"I wonder where his herd is?" she asked. The elephant turned to keep an eye on them but didn't follow.

"We haven't seen any tracks. Maybe he's lost?" As he pulled open the door, the elephant's trunk came over his head and held it open for them.

"It could be he was trained for the tourist trade and now that that has evaporated, his mahout has abandoned him." She gave the elephant a sympathetic look. "Poor thing. He's probably terribly lonely."

He and Malee slipped inside, and the elephant put his head right up to the door.

"Malee, you cannot adopt a stray elephant."

Malee turned and said something to the elephant in Thai. The beast nodded his head as though understanding her words before sitting on his backside. "See, he is trained."

"You still can't keep him. We're temporary here, remember? Can't you tell him to go find his trainer or his herd?"

She spoke again in Thai, even gestured toward the jungle, but the animal didn't move. And there was nothing they could do to get it to leave.

The heavens broke open, and a deluge descended. Water streamed off the elephant, but still the big animal didn't move. Instead, it closed its eyes and seemed to fall back to sleep. Quietly, they closed the door behind them and made their way down the hallway. Caleb kept a tight grip on Malee's hand in the dim light.

"I should start dinner," Malee whispered.

"Don't you want to change first?" Her shirt had dried slightly, but it was still far too easy to see her braless breasts pressed against the fabric.

"I don't have a lot of choice and don't want to ruin my dress by cooking in it."

"I'll lend you a shirt."

They went upstairs while he did a quick mental review of what he'd packed—or rather what his housekeeper had packed. One of his dress shirts would provide the most coverage without clinging to her. He grabbed one out of his bag and handed it to her.

"Are you sure? This looks rather expensive," she said, holding it up to the meager light.

"It's fine, I have dozens more. Are you okay with the

storm?" At her nod, he continued, "I'll meet you in the kitchen in ten minutes?" He was going to use nine of those to remind himself of all the reasons why he couldn't have sex with Malee tonight. It would undoubtedly be a futile effort.

***

An elephant snored at the back door, lights flickered in the hallway like they were in some kind of nightclub fantasy, and the water left behind by the passing thunderstorm dripped from every external surface. A typical evening at Destiny Resort.

Malee suppressed a giggle and made her way to the kitchen. Caleb's shirt came almost to her knees, and the soft cotton fabric caressed her breasts with each movement. Unfortunately, it was freshly laundered so didn't smell like him. She should have asked for one he'd already worn.

If she were philosophical, she'd see the loss of her bra as symbolic—throwing off the shackles of restraint, freeing her to experience more of Caleb's touch. But she wasn't philosophical; she was a realist. And the facts were that in two days, he'd be returning to Canada and she'd still be here, trying to find a job and a way to bring her mother back to Thailand.

When she got to the kitchen, he was leaning against the counter, a glass of wine in his hand. Another glass sat on the stainless-steel worktop next to the bottle. His eyes flared as his gaze swept up and down her body, clad only in his shirt.

"Probably best not to let me near any knives," he said, his voice deep and sultry. He poured wine into the waiting glass and handed it to her.

"Why?" Their fingers grazed as she took the beverage from him.

"Because I'm likely to lop off a finger. I'm not sure I'll be able to concentrate with you wearing that."

"Shall I take it off?" She toyed with the highest button she'd done up.

Caleb's answer was a growl. "Food first. I have a feeling I'm going to need my stamina."

Her laugh came out way huskier than she intended. Who knew she was such a flirt?

Side by side, they prepared the meal, offering tastes to each other as they went. Malee had never shared a kitchen with a man before and found it oddly … satisfying. This is what she wanted in life: a partnership. Something she was unlikely to find in her village, where the custom was still for the woman to do most of the domestic work. Her upbringing in London conflicted with her Thai heritage. Would she ever feel she truly belonged someplace? Someplace other than nestled against Caleb's chest?

They made *khao soi*, a noodle soup dish her mother was famous for. The scent of limes, chilies, and coconut milk filled the air, and by the time they'd finished the preparations, even Malee's stomach was growling. She pulled two bowls off the shelf and gave them a wipe-down. The heat of cooking, combined with Caleb's nearness, had the shirt once again plastered to her skin.

"The rain has stopped. Let's eat outside where it's

cooler," he suggested. The button-down short-sleeved shirt he wore also stuck to his body, outlining his muscles. Now her fingers itched to slip his buttons free and run her hands over his chest. She stifled a groan and grabbed a serving tray from the stash beside the refrigeration unit before she did something she might regret.

Caleb carried their meal outside while Malee grabbed the wine, their glasses, and a couple of dry cushions. The storm had passed, leaving a clear sky and freshly washed air. A perfect evening.

"I'll be right back," Caleb said, disappearing around the back of the hotel again.

He came back holding four small tin buckets and a tall candle under one arm. He placed the miniature buckets around them and lit the citronella candles within. The tall church candle he positioned and lit between them on the table.

"Are the violin players tuning up?"

His laugh echoed through the still night air. "I didn't want you to be afraid of the dark."

She stilled at his words. It was almost dark, but the fear that usually lapped at the edge of her consciousness wasn't there. "Thank you," was all she could manage to say. She hid her confusion with a sip of her wine.

Caleb tasted the meal, his eyes half closing as he removed the spoon from his mouth. "This is excellent."

A movement caught her attention out of the corner of her eye. The elephant had moved soundlessly to stand vigil just beyond the citronella candles.

When it sat on its haunches, Malee began to giggle.

"If it begs for table scraps, I'm going to lose it. Maybe it thinks it's a dog?"

"Trust my luck to have the world's largest mooch chaperone our dinner."

She tilted her head to one side. "A chaperone? Why? What did you have in mind, Mr. Doyle?"

His eyes blazed and a lazy, sexy smile curved his lips. "I have nothing planned. I believe in being spontaneous."

If that included combustion, then so did she.

A large gray trunk flicked over the table. They both snatched up their wineglasses before they were knocked over. The elephant sniffed their dinners but evidently decided that *khao soi* wasn't to his taste, because he then got up and wandered toward the side of the hotel, where they could hear him pulling at the tall grass.

"At least he does the gardening," she said.

"And leaves sizable deposits of fertilizer."

"That's true. But I'm not sure what we can do about it. He seems to have adopted us. We should give him a name."

Caleb leaned across the table and tucked a strand of her hair behind her ear, his fingers caressing her cheek before he sat back. "What would you suggest?"

"Steve," she said.

He almost choked on his soup. "Steve? What kind of elephant name is that?"

"Let me guess: you were going to suggest Dumbo or Babar."

He attempted to hide a smirk behind his wineglass. "I bow to your greater knowledge of elephants. Steve, it is.

But you have to tell him."

Malee stood and nearly tumbled over. She should probably put down her wine and eat some of her dinner. But first, she turned in the direction their newest pet had taken, and called out, "Your name is Steve! And if you need something in the night, be sure to call Caleb and not me!"

"Touché. Now, eat your dinner before Steve comes back and decides that *khao soi* is what he wants. Because I'm not sharing mine."

They both dug in, and within minutes, their bowls were empty. The evening stretched before them long and dark.

"What do you want to do now?" she asked, not sure if she was ready for the answer.

He waggled his eyebrows, and she burst out laughing. If that was his sexy look, then maybe he wasn't the playboy she'd first thought him to be.

"If the dark doesn't bother you, we could do some stargazing," he suggested.

"That sounds wonderful."

"Wait here." He topped up her wineglass, snatched up their empty bowls, and disappeared into the black night.

The candle on the table sputtered out. A niggle of fear slid over her skin, raising gooseflesh. Her pulse pounded in her ears, and the delicious dinner she'd eaten roiled in her stomach. Before she could launch fully into panic mode, Caleb reappeared next to her. He glanced at her face, dropped whatever he'd been carrying, and pulled her into his arms. Her breasts were crushed against his abdomen and her head tucked firmly under his chin. His hands ran up and down her back as though she were cold.

"Sorry. I shouldn't have left you alone."

"It's not your fault." Now her heart was racing, but for an entirely different reason.

She felt him shrug. "It's a Canadian thing. We apologize."

"What did you get?" She pulled out of his embrace, more to show him she was back in control than because she wanted to leave.

"A free-standing hammock. I found it in the storage room this morning. I haven't tested it out, so if it collapses under us, I take no responsibility. But I thought it would be worth a try. The grass is still wet."

"Absolutely."

While he set up the contraption with more than a little swearing, she repositioned the candles around them. In the distance, it sounded like Steve was now pruning the trees bordering the property.

"There. Damn, I should have brought a blanket."

She eyed the hammock. It currently sat only about twenty centimeters high. Add their combined weight to it, and they'd probably be on the ground. Plus, it was barely wide enough for Caleb's body, never mind hers. They'd have to snuggle. Really close.

"It's perfect. And I don't think we'll be cold."

Even in the dim light of the candles, she could see his gaze sweep her body again. "No, I don't think we will. Ladies first."

"How did I get volunteered to be the guinea pig?" But she attempted to get in without further prompting. His shirt rode up as she shifted over, and she was pretty sure he got a good glimpse of a butt cheek in the process.

Caleb sat on the edge of the hammock a moment later, and she rolled right into him. She pushed against his back, attempting to remain on the side of the fabric, but to no avail. When he tried to get his legs on, she flipped out the other side. As she faceplanted into the damp grass, laughter welled up inside her.

"That didn't quite go to plan," Caleb said, peering over the side of the hammock at her.

As she predicted, with Caleb in it, the hammock now barely cleared the ground. And there were mere centimeters of space on either side of him. She put both hands on her hips and checked him out. His arms were folded behind his head, a sexy grin firmly in place. His eyes dared her to join him.

Challenge accepted.

"You leave me no choice. I'm going to climb on top of you. Hang on, this might get bumpy."

"Babe, I'm counting on it."

She was too.

Chapter Nine

So this was fun.

Caleb kept one ear open for sounds of Steve returning from the job he was doing on the landscaping. With both of them in the hammock, his ass was resting on the grass. And the likelihood of being stepped on by their new pet was high on his list of concerns. Not that he'd move, even if he could. Ninety-eight percent of Malee lay on top of him. She had one hip on the hammock's fabric. The rest was plastered to him, and the effort to even get in this position had undone another two buttons on her shirt and made it ride up to the point of indecency.

This had been a brilliant idea.

"I rarely go outside after dark and even then, I don't look up. I didn't realize how many stars you could see here," Malee whispered. Her warm breath slithered down his chest. His arm around her back tightened involuntarily. There were a lot of involuntary reactions occurring around his body.

"Once, when I was working up north, I saw the northern lights. It was spectacular."

"Oh, I'd love to see those. Do you get them in Vancouver?" Her voice was full of awe, with a hint of her native Thai accent slipping through. Would she shed her British tones in the throes of passion? His already hard cock swelled further at the thought. *Down, boy.*

He cleared his throat before he could speak. "On very rare occasions. If you come to Canada, I'll take you up north, where the chances are greater." The invitation had slipped out, but now that he thought about it, it was a good idea. He'd love to show Malee his country, introduce her to his friends, see the city through her eyes.

He felt as much as heard her sigh.

"That's not likely. I need to get a regular job and start making money so my mum isn't supporting the whole family. After all she's done for me, I should be looking after her now."

His hand traced the contour of her spine. She was so small and delicate, yet carried a weighty responsibility. "If the resort were opened, you could work here."

"Yes."

He half expected her to launch into another speech on how the hotel could be made profitable, but she didn't. Instead she rubbed her cheek on his chest, her hand resting on his thigh. His cognitive processes threatened to shut down entirely, a situation not helped by her rock-hard nipples pressing into his chest.

Could he buy it and somehow make it work? It would be a challenge, but he'd never minded hard work before. God knew he had the money. And it would bring so much benefit to the village. And Malee. She could manage the place. Except then she'd truly be his employee, and that wasn't the role he wanted her in. Although exactly what role she should play in his life wasn't clear. "Malee…"

"Let's not talk about it now. Tonight, I just want to be the real me without stressing about my family."

"And what does 'being the real you' involve?"

Her hand moved two centimeters closer to his bulging erection. "Enjoying myself for a change without overthinking things or worrying about the future."

He tilted her face up with a finger under her jaw. He needed to see her expression in the flickering candlelight to know this was what she wanted. "And does enjoying yourself extend beyond looking at the stars?"

She bit down on her bottom lip, but her eyes held his gaze. "I'm hoping I might see some stars indoors as well."

Shifting her body so she lay completely on top of him, he then eased her lip out from between her teeth. "That can definitely be arranged."

He had all night, so he wasn't going to rush this. He'd worship her body, learn her secrets and what pleased her most. Then he'd do it all over again. Their lips touched, and all his good intentions evaporated faster than a drop of water in the Sahara at noon. Their chemistry was too explosive to go slow. At least for the first time.

New plan: wild passion, then a slow exploration.

His hands were one step ahead and already caressed her back under her shirt, slipping to the side so he touched the swell of her breasts. Ever since this afternoon, he'd been dying for another taste of those decadent peaks.

Malee seemed to have the same idea, because suddenly her knees were on either side of his thighs and she'd undone the rest of the buttons on the shirt she wore. He reached out to caress her, but the skin he encountered was wrinkly and felt like an eraser.

"Steve! Not now," Malee said, a sigh of frustration ending her sentence.

"You have got to be kidding me." Caleb managed to leverage himself up without flipping them both off the hammock. His attempts to push Steve's trunk out of the way, however, were futile. The elephant seemed to think they were playing a game, and every time Caleb tried to reach Malee, Steve would block the pass.

"It's probably for the best," Malee said as she re-buttoned her shirt. "You're used to sophisticated women who wear designer clothes and have shoe collections. I'm a country girl who gets her dresses from the second-hand store and owns four pairs of footwear—five if you count my rubber boots."

Steve sat and tilted his head, as though he, too, was interested in Caleb's reply. Two of the citronella candles had been knocked over and extinguished. And dammit, despite Malee's cynical accusation, his first thought was to make sure the enhanced darkness didn't upset her. She scooted back on his thighs so he could sit up.

"Is that what you think of me? That I'm only interested in rich women and I'm just playing with you until I can get back to them?"

"Aren't you? Come on, Caleb. We're from opposite worlds. There's no place in my life for a man like you, and I'm sure I wouldn't fit into your lifestyle either."

She spoke the truth. But it still stung.

"So what was with the whole, 'I just want to be the real me' business? Wasn't that you using me? A little bit of fun while you wait for Mr. Right?" Just saying the words made it feel like Steve was sitting on his chest. He

could not get involved with her. He had his own
company to run, his brother's to rescue, and a hundred
other cliffs and peaks to climb, maybe even Everest one
day. No way could he manage even half of that with
Malee at his side. She came across as a woman who'd
want her husband home at six every day for a hot meal,
a cuddle on the sofa, and long nights of passionate
lovemaking. He sucked in a deep breath to release some
of the pressure on his chest.

Malee climbed off him and managed to make it off
the hammock without faceplanting into the grass again.

"Yes, you're right. You're my little rebellion against
what life has planned for me. You're my adventure, my
cliff." Her accent was back to being crisply British, her
false control betrayed by a slight wobble in her voice.
She took two steps back toward the hotel but stopped.
The moon had slid behind a cloud. The once starry sky
was quickly becoming obscured.

"I don't mind being your adventure, Malee. But
you're wrong if you think I'm just making do with you
while I'm stuck here. I've never kissed a woman just
because she was on hand. I find you far more interesting,
and far sexier, than any designer-dress-clad woman I've
met in recent memory. I'd love to explore your body,
bring you to heights of pleasure. But not as a conquest
or because I need to have sex. I want to because I want
you, Malee Wattana. And I know we would be amazing
together."

She turned back to him then, and it could have been a
trick of the dim light, but he was pretty sure she wiped a
tear off her cheek. "You're a sweet-talker, Caleb Doyle.

Did you practice that fancy patter on your rich girlfriends?"

He took one step toward her and saw the huge grin on her face. "Did you say that hoping I'd throw you over my shoulder and carry you back to the hotel and show you what I think of that statement?"

She shrugged, and his shirt slipped off one shoulder. Why the hell was he still standing there? If she wanted a display of manly brawn, he could give it to her.

"Well, it is very dark. And I didn't want to step in any of Steve's fertilizer."

His laugh bounced off the resort walls and disappeared into the still night. Steve wandered off, clearly not interested in them anymore. "If you wanted me to carry you, you could have asked."

He relit the candle from the table and handed it to her, then put out the other two Steve hadn't knocked over. Scooping her up in his arms, he made sure his left hand had a firm hold on her bare thigh. He was tempted to carry her fireman-style so he could enjoy her delectable ass on the way. But the beauty of her face would then be wasted. Besides, he needed her to hold the candle to light their way.

"Wait," she said before he'd taken two steps.

"Did you forget something?" The wine bottle was empty and the glasses could stay where they were until morning. Any intrepid ants that found them could get drunk on the dregs.

"I want to see the fireflies."

Oh God. She wasn't intoxicated, was she? He couldn't take advantage of a drunk woman. "What fireflies?"

"Down by the waterfall. My mother told me about them. But I've always been too scared of the dark to go see them."

"It's still dark."

"Yes, but I'm not scared when I'm with you." She'd wrapped an arm around his neck, and her fingers toyed with the hair at his nape. Desire stirred again in his groin. He should carry her into the hotel. They could go in search of fireflies tomorrow night.

But he turned toward the path down to the water anyway. He couldn't see more than two feet ahead. If Steve was lying down, they'd probably fall right on top of him. But given that the beast had interrupted their make-out session earlier, he deserved to be trodden on.

"This is insanity, you know that, don't you? The likelihood of my falling and both of us winding up with broken bones is high. And what if the candle goes out?"

If he thought that would sway her, he was sadly mistaken.

"Come on, where's your sense of adventure now?"

Upstairs in my room, waiting to get you naked.

***

She was stalling. She knew it. Caleb undoubtedly knew it too. It wasn't that she didn't want to make love with him. She did. God, so much. But what if it was as spectacular as in one of her romance novels? How would any other man compete after that? How could she settle for normal if he gave her amazing?

So here they were. She was perched on Caleb's thighs, and he was sitting on a rock beside the waterfall's pool, watching a bunch of bugs light up their butts.

"I've never seen so many fireflies in one location," Caleb whispered into her ear.

His warm breath slid down her cleavage, putting her nipples on high alert. Enough of the delay tactics. She needed to absorb some of his courage and seize the day, or rather the man.

Maybe it wasn't courage she needed, but a bit of recklessness. Or to bloody well stop over-thinking this. So what if she'd only met Caleb three days ago? Their chemistry had been instantaneous.

"Did you know that the adult firefly's sole purpose is to procreate?" Her voice came out breathy. Hopefully he wouldn't notice.

"Lucky firefly." Caleb's hand at her waist slid up her back and played with her hair for a moment before making the return journey. His touch left a trail of quivering flesh in its wake. And that was with fabric between his hand and her skin.

"Maybe we should take a lesson from the brilliant bug, if you'll excuse the pun."

This time, his hand moved around and ran up her side, lingering for a long moment on the side of her breast. "I'm not sure I can let that one go. You may need to be *pun*ished."

She slid off his lap and stood before him. "It was a pretty minor offense. What does my correction entail?"

"Undo two—no, make that three—buttons on your shirt."

She slid the small plastic disks through the fabric. His gaze was riveted on her chest, although what he could see in the dim light was questionable. The moon continued to play hide and seek with the clouds. When she'd finished with the last button, he slipped his hand inside to caress her breast. A moan of pleasure escaped her lips.

His thumb flicked over her pebbled nipple twice before he took it between his fingers and rolled it. Her knees weakened, and she clutched his shoulders for support. God, she was such a lightweight when it came to seduction.

One of her hands slid from his shoulder into his hair and pulled his head toward her chest. She wanted his mouth on her again more than she wanted to breathe.

His tongue darted out and flicked one nipple, while his hand continued to explore the other breast. "Let's go back to the hotel," he said against her chest. "I don't want to be interrupted by Steve again. Plus, unlike fireflies, we need to be concerned with conception. I don't have a condom with me."

She nodded dumbly, although it was doubtful he saw. Despite his words, he made another leisurely pass over her breast with his lips. When her knees turned to jelly, he released her nipple from his mouth and stood.

Grabbing the candle, the flame immediately went out, leaving them in total darkness. Caleb wrapped his strong arms around her and whispered into the top of her head, "Are you okay?"

Surprisingly, she was. "Fine. Let's go." She took his hand and they made their way over to the cement steps leading up to the hotel. As she lifted her foot to access the first stair, the rock on which her other foot stood shifted under her weight. Had it not been for Caleb's lightning reaction, she would have fallen.

"Thanks," she said. She needed to concentrate on walking and not the sensation of the night air slipping over her nipples, still damp from his mouth. However, when she went to take another step, her ankle completely gave way. Her cry of pain sliced through the dark. Caleb quickly scooped her up in his arms.

Thankfully, the moon came out from behind the clouds as they ascended the steps and then walked across the lawn. Steve lay sleeping, and snoring, on top of the now-destroyed hammock. Caleb flipped on the lights inside the hotel, setting her down in the reception area while he secured the doors for the night. "Don't put any weight on that ankle until I've had a chance to look at it," he said.

Despite his words, she tentatively tested it, only to have pain shoot up her leg. To mask her disobedience, she lounged against the reception desk. The spider that had once lived there had been relocated outside earlier in the day.

"There's a first-aid kit in the kitchen," she said. Hopefully she'd just twisted it and would quickly recover.

While he went to get the kit, Malee hopped the few steps to the stairs, but he caught up with her before she could get too far. "Hey, take it easy." Once more he lifted her effortlessly and carried her to his room. "You're going to have to stay off that ankle for the rest of the night, and it would be better if you were in here, in case you need anything," he said at her raised eyebrow.

"My ankle. Yeah, that's why I'm in your room."

He placed her gently on the bed and pulled his shirt off over his head like he couldn't wait a minute longer to get naked. "Did you want to register a formal protest?"

"No."

She lay back as he gently examined her ankle, his fingers causing more havoc in her brain than pain in her lower leg.

"How does it feel?" he asked.

"A bit tender."

His green eyes blazed, and he pressed against her skin a couple more times. She could feel it swelling but was too distracted by the sight of Caleb's strong fingers against her skin to complain.

"It doesn't feel broken, so it's probably just a sprain. To be safe, I think we should wrap it. And you've got a bit of mud on you. I'd better clean that off." He activated a chemical ice pack and lay it on her ankle while he went to get some water and a flannel. When he returned, he stood next to the bed and stared down at her for a good thirty seconds.

"Something wrong?" she asked.

"No, for once, I think everything might be all right." There was an odd note in his voice, and she propped herself up on her elbows, forgetting that the shirt she wore was mostly unbuttoned and revealing almost all her breasts. Caleb hauled in a deep breath before adding, "Even better than all right."

He sat carefully on the bed and placed her foot on his

thigh. If she could move her ankle more, she'd be able to trace the erection straining against his shorts with her toe. He gently wiped her lower leg and started to apply the tensor bandage. "You've done this before," she said as he expertly wrapped her ankle.

"I've had a few sprains myself." He clipped the bandage together and ran his hands up the back of her calf, over her knee, and along her lower thigh. "How does that feel now?"

"Better." She closed her eyes and lay back on the bed again. To match the elephant outside, there was one in the room, one that needed addressing before they could go further. "Um, just so you know, I'm not a virgin," she said.

"Okay." He gave no hint as to whether her statement surprised him or not.

"I, uh, had a boyfriend, back in London. We did it a couple of times. But it wasn't very good." Caleb kept silent. Was he reevaluating his desire for her? "He said I was too … stiff."

"Stiff?" The word came out kind of strangled, but his face was completely neutral.

"You know, like a board. The other word he used was *frigid.*"

"Neither of those are words I'd associate with you. But if you're having second thoughts…" He removed his hand from where it had been massaging her calf muscles above her sore ankle.

"No, I want… With you, I don't feel stiff. In fact, I'm kind of melty."

"Melty? I like that. Tell you what. Let's carry on with

our initial non-plan, but if at any time—and I mean *any* time—you want to stop, just say so. I won't think less of you. Or more, for that matter. This is just us … being us … together."

He bent down to kiss her, his lips toying with hers while his hand reached higher up her thigh, a finger grazing the juncture between her leg and body. Then it was gone. Her moan of disappointment was replaced with a gasp of desire as he massaged up her uninjured leg. This time when his hand reached the apex of her thighs, it lingered there. His thumb bypassed her panties and slid between her folds in an erotic tease.

His lips made their way over to her ear. "So wet already. Do you want me to touch you there, Malee?"

"Yes."

Her hips followed his thumb up, desperate to keep his digit in contact with her skin.

"Where else do you want me to touch you? Kiss you?" Another finger joined his thumb, and with his other hand he released the last of the buttons keeping her shirt closed.

"Um, I don't know." He'd pulled her shirt open so her chest was exposed to the dim light of the bedside lamp, but he made no move to touch her breasts.

"Not good enough. I have to know what you want. This is your chance, babe, to get everything you desire."

Wasn't he just supposed to take off her underwear, enter her now, and thrust? Heaven knew he had an erection he could fly a flag from.

"I don't know what I want." All of him, right now, was about all she could think.

"Nope." He took his hands off her body and sat back on his haunches between her knees. "I want instructions. The more explicit the better."

"You got that bit about me not being very experienced, didn't you?"

"Yup. But you're not naïve. I'm sure you've read things … seen things. You may enjoy it more if you get what you want."

She nodded and swallowed twice before she could form the words. "I want you to touch my breasts," she said, heart in mouth.

"Sit up first." She did so, and he propped all the pillows behind her so she was semi-reclined. "You'll need to see what I'm doing so you can tell me what's next," he said.

Oh. God.

He took a breast in each hand as though weighing them. She'd often been annoyed at their size before. Larger than most women of her height and frame, she'd been plagued with backaches and the need to buy specialty bras. For the first time in her life, her breasts were exactly right.

"Run your thumb over one nipple while you suck on the other," she instructed. She barely recognized her own voice, it was so breathy.

He obeyed instantly and Malee threw her head back, closing her eyes on the pleasure.

"Keep watching," Caleb commanded. Her head snapped up as he switched sides. The ache in her core, the need for his touch down there, was more intense than she'd ever experienced before.

"Could you—?"

"No requests. I want commands, Malee."

"I thought you didn't like being told what to do."

His smile was … wolfish. "I'm making an exception for you. I'll take orders for the next hour. Then we switch roles."

An hour? She'd be lucky to be able to breathe for another ten minutes. The tension inside her was already approaching critical levels.

"Touch my clit," she said in the most commanding voice she could manage at this point in time. It came out a husky plea. But it must've been good enough, since he complied. Her hips rocked up, but when she put weight on her injured ankle, she gasped. The shot of pain was short-lived, however, as her nervous system was currently dealing with a barrage of pleasure messages.

"We should probably elevate your ankle," Caleb said. He lifted her leg and put it over his shoulder. His eyes caught and held hers, and his green eyes darkened with passion. "Have you ever had your clit licked?"

"No."

"Would you like that?"

"I'm not sure."

"I'll head in that direction, and if you don't like it, then tell me to stop." The heat in his gaze raised her core temperature to critical.

His tongue did a couple laps around her belly button before heading over to her hip bone. She was melting beneath him, the exquisite sensations exploding throughout her body. He'd said he didn't mind being her adventure. And dammit, for once she was going to seize the moment.

"Oh God, Caleb, that feels so good." He blew cool air against the overheated skin of her drenched folds, sending her nerve endings into a frenzy.

"What do you want me to do, Malee?" His teeth nipped the tender flesh of her upper thigh before his tongue swirled around the love bite. She shivered in anticipation of his next move.

"Carry on?" Her brain was having enough trouble keeping up with what he was doing now. No way could she plan the next move.

"Explicit details. Tell me what you want." He shifted so his head was between her thighs, waiting for the order. The passion and adoration in his eyes as they met hers emboldened her.

"I want the indoor stars, Caleb. Take me with your tongue. Make me scream your name."

All he had to do was touch her once, and she came apart.

She was never going to recover from this night.

Chapter Ten

Boneless. There was no other way to describe how she felt. She'd come so many times, she'd lost count. On his tongue… With him inside her, him on top… On her knees with him behind… So many things she'd fantasized about had been enacted in explicit glory. Caleb, however, seemed to sense where her boundaries were and never pushed her beyond them. But everything right up to the line was exquisite.

Now they lay with her tucked against his side, her head on his chest, his hand stroking along her back as though he couldn't touch her enough.

"You didn't get your hour of control," she said when her voice had finally recovered from screaming his name.

"I had too much fun taking orders from you. I'll take my turn tomorrow. Besides, I don't think I could go again just yet."

She shifted her arm so it lay across his abdomen, and his hand now ran up her side, whispering over the side of her breast before heading back down again. With the rhythmic caress and the activity of the past few hours, her eyelids were struggling to stay open. But she didn't want to sleep yet, didn't want to let go of the moment.

"Tell me about your family," she said.

His hand stopped moving and for a second, she feared

he would move away.

"Not much to tell. My dad died when I was twenty. Before that, he was a workaholic and never around, so it wasn't much of a loss. My brother Ian is eight years older than me and married with two children, a boy and girl. My mother is what you'd call a socialite. Her sole purpose in life is to be seen at the right events, wearing the right clothes."

His cold assessment of the people who should have been the most important in his life left her chilled. "It sounds as though you don't like your family much." She reached behind for the sheet to cover her body. The warm glow of Caleb's lovemaking had diminished.

"I neither like nor dislike them. Some people have dysfunctional families—mine is more ambivalent. I've never had much in common with Ian. He's like my father was and stuck in the old ways of doing things. I'm all about innovation and trying new things, whereas he's a traditionalist. Sarah, his wife, is very nice. She's quiet and calm and a great mother, really involved in her children's school and life."

"And your mother wasn't?"

"No. Not that I remember, anyway. She's always done her own thing, even when my father was alive. If I didn't have money to fund her way of life, I'm pretty sure I'd never hear from her."

"Maybe she feels invisible. It probably started long ago, when you were a kid, and now she doesn't know any other way to reach you. You said your dad was a workaholic—he obviously ignored her. And it sounds like you and your brother both have busy lives that don't include her. Everyone wants to be seen, to be acknowledged, to be appreciated, Caleb. Maybe her asking you for money is the only way she can get your attention."

"I… I would go to dinner with her, if she asked." He seemed doubtful about his own statement.

"I'm sorry for you." Even though her mother had worked two jobs when Malee had first arrived in the UK, Mum had still made time for them to do fun stuff. Even if it was just a walk in the park to kick leaves and collect horse chestnuts.

"Why? I grew up with anything I wanted. I was popular. I had few restrictions. Harrison, my friend, has a close-knit family, and they always welcomed me at the dinner table. So whenever I wanted a family fix, I'd just go over there."

"See, rather than turn to your own family for support, you used your friend's." She shrugged. "I guess that's one big difference between Canada and Thailand. In Thai culture, family is all-important."

"And if your family is a dud, like mine?"

"Then you work harder to build the relationships. You don't get to choose your family."

"What about your cousin—Bodin, isn't it? Are you telling me you have a close relationship with him when he tells you off in front of other people?"

"In every family, there are favorites and ones you'd rather never see again. And for all Bodin's faults, I can understand where he's coming from. He's a true local. As far as I'm aware, he's never been farther from the village than Chiang Rai. Then I come home. I'm more educated, have seen more of the world, I'm able to communicate with you easily. He couldn't rescue us. He feels his position as head of the family is under threat. In his mind, he's left me to your mercy. He reacted by chastising me in front of the villagers to show he's still in charge."

"I didn't like it. And his ideas are antiquated. You're an amazing woman: smart, funny, and you know more about water buffalo than anyone other than a vet should…"

She groaned. "You're not going to forget that, are you?"

"Never." He kissed the top of her head. "My point is that your cousin, someone who knows you better than me, should be able to see your good qualities as well. Anyone who doesn't should be cut from your life so you don't start to doubt yourself."

"Change takes time. You can't abandon those who belong to you but who take longer to adjust. Like your brother. He probably doesn't know any other way to do business. You're obviously brilliant—you should help him."

"I am helping him. I'm here, aren't I?"

"And when you get home?"

"I'll … do what I can."

She nodded, although she wasn't sure if he was telling the truth. "What about a family of your own some day— a wife and children?" That probably wasn't the question to ask when she was lying naked next to him.

"I have no plans to marry. You said yourself that if I had a wife and children who depended on me, I wouldn't be able to do any of the reckless things I enjoy."

"Maybe one day you'll meet a woman who's more important to you than any adventure." Her heartbeat stuttered, and an emptiness opened inside her, waiting for his answer.

"Perhaps. But at this moment, I'm not interested in the future. I'm all about the here and now." His hand resumed its slow caress over her skin again. She concentrated on the trail of tingles left by his touch, ignoring both the throbbing of her ankle and the ache in her heart that she wouldn't be the woman to tempt Caleb into giving up his thrill seeking.

"The here and now is pretty fine," she acknowledged as his bristly jaw rubbed against the side of her breast and he explored her torso with his lips.

"Fine?" He raised his head, his green eyes alight with laughter. "I must be doing this wrong. I'm aiming for epic."

If this was all she was going to get from the man, she'd take it. "By all means, then, make it epic."

And he did.

***

Caleb watched the dust motes dance in the early morning sunlight. He'd had other things on his mind last night than closing the curtains. Malee was snuggled against his side, and he was loath to move and disturb her. They'd achieved epic status. It'd been some of the best sex he'd ever had. Whatever guy had told Malee she was stiff and frigid had clearly been an ass. He smiled. Or an arse, as she would say.

Yup, it had been a night to remember. Except when she'd been harping on about his family. Or a possible future one. He'd been avoiding that idea all his adult life, imagining that he was genetically predisposed to selfishness, which, from what he'd seen, was not conducive to a happy marriage. But lying here with a warm, caring woman in his arms, all he wanted was to make her happy.

Was it just post-sex euphoria? The terror and run-for-the-hills urge he normally associated with thoughts of marriage were just a faint niggle. Sure, the night with Malee had been spectacular, but that could be attributed to the forty-eight hours of foreplay. He'd never worked so hard or taken so long to seduce a woman before. It was the victory after a long-fought battle that had made it special. Although that didn't account for his intense desire to take her over and over again until neither of them could move.

Or maybe it was this place that was magical. From his late teens, he'd always had an internal itch to push himself to the limits. He'd noticed that last night and again this morning, that sensation was gone. It was as though he'd finally found what he'd been searching for. And it wasn't adventure or a new thrill—it was a woman and a place far removed from the life he normally led.

Too bad he couldn't stay. He had obligations. And despite his affirmation last night that he felt no familial connection, he couldn't let his brother, or the family company, go to the wall. His life was in Vancouver, and Malee had already said she had no desire to leave northern Thailand. Which gave them approximately thirty hours to enjoy each other. How many of those could he spend making love to her?

He wasn't sure what his housekeeper thought he got up to on business trips, but she'd packed two boxes of condoms in his suitcase. For once, he applauded Mrs. Levy's overabundance of optimism.

Malee stirred in his arms, and he shifted so he would be the first thing she saw when she opened her eyes. Jesus, now he was becoming a romantic.

"Hey," he said, because the words on the tip of his tongue were impossible. *Let's never leave.*

"Morning." She shifted some more and winced.

"How's the ankle?"

"Sore." Her gaze slid away from his.

"And the rest of you?"

Her brown eyes snapped back to his. "If you're asking if I regret last night, the answer is no. It was amazing. Thank you."

He attempted a casual shrug. "It's the least I could do to take your mind off your ankle."

Her light laugh did more to reassure him than her words. "I appreciate your efforts. I definitely was not thinking about my ankle last night." She flung back the sheet and lifted her leg into a shaft of sunlight. Her lower leg resembled an overstuffed sausage. "I'll soak it in cold water later. That should help bring down the swelling."

"I'll bring the water to you. You are spending the day in bed."

A sensuous smile curved her lips. "Is that a doctor's

orders or a lover's?"

"Whatever it takes to keep you off your ankle." He fought a smile but lost the battle. "And naked."

"I'm not sure being naked will help my ankle."

"Do you not remember last night?"

She laughed, and his heart lightened. "If I say no, will that get me a repeat performance?"

"All you need to do for that is ask." He rolled so he was leaning over her. As he ran the tip of his tongue along the underside of her jaw, a loud trumpet blast from their resident elephant interrupted his exploration. Damn, he'd been hoping that Steve would have wandered off in the night. Not that he had anything against the pachyderm. Steve just diverted Malee's attention from himself. *See, selfishness is in my blood.*

Malee pushed on his shoulder. God, he'd never had a woman in his bed who wanted to talk so much. "When we get out of here, I'll try to find Steve's mahout."

"And what are you going to do if you find him? You can't force the person to take Steve back. And what if his mahout was abusing him? Would you return him to a life of pain?"

"I don't know. I'll deal with the situation when I get all the facts. At the moment, all I see is that he's obviously trained, and elephants go through hell during the training process. I hate to think that humans put him through that and then just abandoned him when things got tough."

He trailed a finger along her jaw. "You have a beautiful heart, Malee."

A faint blush darkened her skin tone. "Thanks. Last

night you told me I had a beautiful ass when you took me from behind. I'll take both compliments with the same sentiment." She threw back the covers and scooted out the other side of the bed. She let out a yelp of pain as she put weight on her ankle and collapsed back onto the bed.

He raced around and helped her stand. "And what sentiment would that be?"

"That you want my body." A frown tugged his lips down before he could stop them. Malee reached up and smoothed the lines on his forehead before dropping a sweet kiss on his cheek. "Don't worry. I want your body too, so we're even."

If only it could stay as simple as that.

***

The hammock was beyond repair, so that night they lay on a blanket on the grass. A few meters away, Steve lay on his side, snoring. He'd tried to get on the blanket as well, but a firm command to move back and stay had the animal retreating a respectful distance. He'd dogged their steps all day, but at least had made no more efforts to get between them.

Malee had refused to stay in bed, and he'd had to admit, it was too hot and stuffy to make love all day. There was unfortunately not enough electricity to run the air conditioners. So he'd carried her down to the waterfall so she could soak her ankle, which had immediately reduced the swelling. They'd frolicked in the water, ended up naked, and made love on a ledge behind the waterfall. Then they'd sunbathed, which had more to do with Caleb's desire to rub cream all over Malee's already-dark skin than a desire to get a tan himself. Of course, that had led to other things, and alfresco sex had then necessitated the need for another washing off. During a brief and thankfully light rain storm, they'd retreated to the bedroom. While Malee had napped for an hour, he'd spent the time trying to convince himself that this thing between them had to end in Thailand.

Was it just his hero complex taking over? She certainly made him feel like the most special man in the world. But it wasn't narcissism driving him. He wanted to be there for her, no matter what.

When she'd woken from her sleep, he'd had his hour of control, but found he'd enjoyed it more when Malee had been issuing the tentative commands. Helping her discover her sensuality, which, as he'd guessed, had lain dormant—waiting for the right moment, or the right man, to release her inner temptress—had been more satisfying than any previous orgasm he'd had. He was fast developing an addiction to her that he was sure would end with agonizing withdrawals.

"What color are the northern lights, and do they really dance?" Malee had her head on his shoulder, their fingers entwined between them. She'd not had a single panic attack since nightfall, although he'd been careful to stay near and keep one of the gas lights close by. Candles might be more romantic, but they were too volatile. This was practical romance.

"The ones I've seen in Vancouver are mostly green.

But up north, they shimmer and change from green to blue to red sometimes. It's one of those things I think you could see a thousand times and never take for granted." Kind of like kissing her. Each time was profoundly satisfying and just as amazing.

"Are you looking forward to going home?"

"No. But I can't stay here. I have responsibilities. This has been fabulous, but it's time to get back to real life. I'll have the helicopter take us to Chiang Mai, and we can stay in a hotel there with running water and flush toilets while I contact the seller. If he doesn't respond within twenty-four hours, I'll return to Canada."

She tried to disguise the shiver that swept through her, but he wasn't fooled. Despite whatever pep talks she'd given herself, she'd clearly become emotionally invested in this affair as well. The only way he would cope with their parting would be to bury himself in work. Oddly enough, the idea of scaling a cliff or doing some other extreme sport held no appeal.

"And if the seller responds, what will you do?"

He could hear the hopeful note in her voice. He hated to quash her dreams, but stringing her along wouldn't help either of them. "If he's willing to sell for what my brother has already deposited, then we'll conclude negotiations. I'll then talk to Ian when he's fully recovered, and we'll go from there. If the seller insists on his original asking price, then we walk away and initiate legal proceedings to get our money back. I believe we have a pretty good case for misrepresentation, given the state of the place."

"Then Destiny Resort remains a dream."

There was quashing dreams, and there was crushing them and setting them alight. "For now. One thing I've learned in business is to never say never." He rolled to his side so he could stare down into her face. Her lips were slightly parted as though waiting for his kiss. Or was that just wishful thinking? "Malee—"

She put a finger on his lips. "Don't, Caleb. I know what you're going to say, and I've been telling myself the same thing all day long. It's been great, but this has to end here."

"Actually, I was about to say that I don't want it to end here. We'll find a way."

Shiiit. Where the hell had that come from?

Chapter Eleven

Just like two days previous, she and Caleb stood on one side of the landslide, and her cousin Bodin and a dozen other villagers were arranged on the other. It was the beginning of the end. She should have been excited, but she wasn't. Although she could do with a few more clothes, the time she'd had alone with Caleb would be something she'd forever remember.

She'd taken his comments about wanting to continue their affair with the skepticism of a woman who'd been promised things before. Once he was back in his world, he'd forget about his little holiday fling, especially if he didn't buy the resort to remind him. For her, she feared, it would be the benchmark against which she compared all future relationships.

"A helicopter will arrive at noon," Bodin said in Thai, while Malee translated for Caleb, who stood next to her. Not touching, but close enough. "And the government heard that a rich businessman had been stranded here and agreed to pay for the road to be rebuilt, starting next week."

Caleb raised an eyebrow but said nothing on that point. "Tell him that we'll be waiting for the helicopter, that we'll go to Chiang Mai. I'll conclude my business in Thailand and then..." His eyes caught hers. "I'll make sure you're returned home safely within a few days, if that's still what you want."

She forced a smile past the ache in her chest and turned back to the chasm to translate the message for those on the other side.

"Cousin," Bodin called out as Caleb moved over to the side of the road, bending to look at something on the ground. "Don't translate this. What's the story on the resort? Is he going to buy it?"

Malee tipped her head to the side, wondering why Bodin was so concerned. A shiver of unease crept over her skin, raising gooseflesh. Although Caleb had said she was technically not working until they met with the sellers, it didn't feel right not to keep him informed of all the discussions.

Her cousin was taking the village's welfare too far. They'd survived for decades without the resort. They'd muddle through somehow. "Doubtful. It's in bad shape and not worth the money being asked. Why?"

"You have to convince him to buy it. Come on, Malee, use some of that womanly charm you've been endowed with. He's loaded, he can afford it. What have you been doing the past two days if not convincing him of Thailand's delights?"

Anger choked her words for a moment then released them in a flood. "I have shown him around, but he's a businessman. He's not going to make an important decision like this based on sentimentality. And your comment about my womanly charms is two-faced when you warned me not to get physically involved with him last time we spoke." She was done being the respectful doormat. Her cousin couldn't stand there, suggest she seduce someone in front of other village men, and get away with it.

He said something to the others she couldn't hear, but she wasn't surprised when they drove off, leaving Bodin alone on the other side.

"Malee, you have to convince him to buy the resort." This was new: Bodin pleading with her. He usually issued commands or spoke sarcastically about her fears.

"Why? What's it to you? Yes, the villagers could do with the work the resort would bring, but you have your own business."

"I borrowed money and bought the place three months ago when I heard there was foreign interest. I can't pay the carrying costs on the loan. If your Mr. Moneybags doesn't buy the hotel, I'll have to sell the store. Think of Suri and the children, Malee. We'll have to leave. And Bodin Jr. has bad lungs. You know how the pollution makes him sick."

Argh! She wanted to pull her hair out. Or punch her cousin in the face. How could he put her in this position? "I have no influence over Caleb's decisions," she said.

"I see the way he watches you." They both turned their heads to where Caleb was kneeling next to the cliff face. As predicted, he was following their exchange with interest. "If you wanted, you could get him to do anything."

"Everything okay, Malee?" Caleb asked.

"Fine. Just getting caught up on some family stuff."

"Please, Cousin. Talk to him."

"I make no promises, Bodin." She'd have to make one more try to get Caleb to buy the place. Not for Bodin. He could wallow in his disgrace for all she cared. But his wife Suri was one of the sweetest people Malee knew, and their children were too young to face this kind of upheaval. "How much did you pay?" Maybe she could get Caleb to settle for a little more than the ten thousand he'd already paid.

"Fifty thousand. I borrowed the money from Mr. Namwiset."

Brilliant. Her cousin was in debt up to his wazoo with a notorious loan shark. "Why the hell are you asking a million, then? You could double your money with just a hundred grand. You knew the state the place was in. How on earth did you think it was worth that much?"

"The seller told me he had three parties interested and was sure there would be a bidding war. Plus, with all the tension in Europe, people are coming back to Asia for holidays. Besides, your Caleb Doyle is loaded. I took the message to Chiang Rai and looked him up on the internet there. He's got way more money than his brother. A million is nothing to him."

"Just because he has the money doesn't mean he's going to waste it."

Bodin's shifty eyes once more moved to Caleb. When he turned his gaze back to Malee, there was a calculating gleam in it she'd never seen before. "He would for you."

"Now you're being completely ridiculous. He's not in love with me or anything like that."

"Then you need to try harder. I'll cut you in on some of the profit. You can use the money to bring your mother home."

"That's not fair." She crossed her arms over her chest

to stop her hands from shaking. He couldn't ask this of her. "What about the other bidders? Have you been in contact with them?"

"I'm beginning to suspect they were fictional. Mr. Caleb or Doyle Destinations is our only chance to survive." Bodin held out his arms. "It's all up to you, Malee. My life, that of my wife and kids, it's all in your hands."

***

Sunlight winked on something metallic near the edge of the landslide. Caleb went to investigate while Malee had a rather earnest discussion with her cousin in Thai. Based on her body language, she was being subjected to more verbal abuse. He wanted to leap across the chasm and pound some twenty-first-century respect for women into her cousin. But he couldn't do that. Not only physically but philosophically. It wasn't his culture. He had no right to interfere.

Malee had to handle this herself. The only thing he could do was remove himself as far as possible from the situation and then reinforce to her later how incredible he found her. Because she was—incredible, fascinating, intelligent, funny, enchanting, and so damn sexy, his cock stirred just looking at her.

How was he was going to let her go in a few days' time? How he could keep them together? Destiny Resort was certainly having a laugh at his expense. He should call it Jackass Resort. Because no matter which way he sliced it, that's how he'd behaved. He'd taken advantage of her and led them both down a path with only heartache at the end.

There was nothing he could do about it now, however, so he turned his attention back to searching for whatever had caught his eye earlier. It was snuggled up against the hillside, almost covered in red mud, just a glimmer of metal reflecting the light.

He carefully extricated it, but there wasn't much buried. It hadn't been there long. The edges weren't rusted, and the label, despite having been subjected to all the recent rain, was still legible.

It was a blasting cap.

What was an explosive doing near the edge of the landslide? Had it been deliberately triggered? By whom? Why? Malee had told people in the village that she was heading to the resort with him on the first day. Had someone wanted them to be stranded there? To what end?

He turned again to Malee and her cousin. The other villagers had left, so their discussion couldn't just be bluster—Bodin asserting his role of family head for their sake. Malee kept shifting her weight and fiddling with her hair until she anchored her hands under her armpits. Meanwhile the man had kept his hands fisted at his side, but his gaze had darted continuously between Caleb and Malee. Was he trying to determine the nature of their relationship? If Caleb had to guess, based on the pleading tone of her cousin's voice and Malee's nervous reply, he was attempting to get her to do something she wasn't happy about.

Caleb pocketed the blasting cap and went to stand by

his woman. In reality, she was only his woman temporarily. The ache in his chest intensified. It took all his self-control not to wrap his arms around her waist and pull her against his chest to ease the pain.

Bodin said one more thing, got back in his Jeep, and reversed at a reckless speed, clearly not waiting for Malee's reply.

Caleb ran a hand down her arm. "What all that was about?"

"My cousin was just … reminding me of the importance of family. Come on. If the helicopter is coming at noon, we have to get going. I'd like to leave the resort in the same shape we found it." She looked like she'd been punched in the gut by whatever her relative had said.

Caleb forced aside his unease and focused on making her feel better. He tucked a stray strand of hair behind her ear. "The same way we found it? About to fall down? Do you plan to put the cobwebs and spiders back?"

She smiled at his jest. "You know what I mean."

"I know I'd enjoy one more visit to the waterfall."

Her eyes turned misty. "Me too. But I don't think we have time for that."

Time. That was one thing his money couldn't buy.

***

"Your cousin seemed upset," Caleb said as they parked once more in front of the hotel. "Everything okay with your family?"

"Fine."

She didn't meet his eyes.

His gaze drifted to their pet elephant waiting patiently by the back door. He had to give it to Steve—he earned his keep doing the gardening. "Did anyone know anything about Steve's mahout?"

Still her gaze didn't meet his. "Sorry, I forgot to ask."

"Malee, if you don't want to come to Chiang Mai with me, I can arrange for you to be taken directly back to your grandparents' house."

That finally brought her face up to his. "No. I want to stay with you for as long as possible."

Maybe that's what was bothering her: the end of their affair. He'd lain awake most of the night thinking about how they could keep in touch. He had the money to jet back and forth between Canada and Thailand, but not the time. Ian's company was going to take a lot of restructuring, which would undoubtedly require site visits to determine which hotels were worth keeping and which could be liquidated. Not to mention his own venture capital company that was busier than ever.

It was time for Caleb to take on a partner, and there was no better candidate than his friend Harrison. The only question was whether the reserved lawyer had it in his nature to take a risk. At least, given his past, he was unlikely to be distracted by a woman, which was Caleb's current dilemma.

"That's good news on the government agreeing to fix the road, isn't it?" she said as they walked arm in arm toward the hotel.

Steve trotted over to them and greeted them with a trumpet blast. They'd be lucky if he hadn't shattered any of the windows with the noise.

"We discussed this before, babe. An access road is the least of the resort's deficiencies."

"You still don't think it's worth more than the ten grand your brother already paid?"

In memories? It was priceless. But he'd never been ruled by sentimentality, so why start now? Although... "No. Even at ten grand, it's overpriced, but it wouldn't be worth the lawyers' fees to try and get more money back. Unless there's fraud involved. I'll have to ask Ian exactly what state he was told the place was in."

Malee kicked a small flower that lined the path. "I see." She hauled in a deep breath and forced a smile on her face. "I'll go to the kitchen and make sure everything is put back and clean."

Sensing she needed a few minutes alone, he let her go. But once they were in Chiang Mai, he'd get her to tell him what had upset her.

It took only twenty minutes to secure all the doors and windows and replace the dust coverings. There was no way to wash the bedsheets, so they folded them up and put them in a bag at the bottom of the laundry cupboard.

As they closed the back door for the last time, a wave of regret pulsed through Caleb. For God's sake, Destiny Resort wasn't his destiny. Mountains, cliff faces, waterfalls: that's what called to him. Except at the thought of waterfalls, he remembered making love to Malee behind the one at the bottom of the path. The cold had peaked her nipples, and he'd sucked them in his mouth until they were warm again. But nothing could diminish the heat of her core as she welcomed him, her legs circling his waist. The curtain of water had shielded them from the outside world until nothing mattered but the woman in his arms and making her his.

"We'd better go," Malee said, staring up at the sun as if it told her the time. His watch was somewhere buried in his bag, his phone battery had died after the first day, and he hadn't missed either. "What about the car?"

"When the road is rebuilt, they can send someone to fetch it. I'll reimburse the rental company for the loss of the vehicle until then. How's your ankle? Are you going to be able to make the climb?" He was clutching at straws now. Maybe they couldn't leave for a few days yet. He'd go up to the helicopter, get them to return with a few more provisions. Then they could come back in a day or two, or a week or two, or a year or two.

"It's fine now. Almost back to normal." Malee circled her foot as if to prove her point and slung her small bag over her shoulder, probably so she could have both hands free in case she slipped. For the first time since he'd arrived, there'd been no thunderstorm storm yesterday, only a brief rain shower. And today, a cooling breeze eased some of the humidity from the air. The path up to the helipad was more discernible, since Malee had hacked away at it previously with the machete. But if he hadn't known what to look for, he'd have passed it by.

How long until any trace of their stay was obliterated by nature? A week? Two? Whereas his time here would stay with him forever. God, when had he become such a sentimentalist? He could just imagine Ian's and Harrison's reactions if he told them he'd bought the place because he'd had the best nights of his life there.

Five minutes up the path, Steve came crashing behind them.

"No, Steve, you can't come with us," he said, trying to shoo the elephant away.

Malee turned around, and a forced giggle escaped her lips. "Ah, Caleb, can't we keep him? Please?"

Steve nodded his head as if agreeing with Malee's question.

"He won't fit in the helicopter." Why was he even having this conversation? It was a damn elephant, and he was leaving, never to return. A sharp stab of pain sliced through his chest.

"Steve." Malee spoke to the elephant in Thai, and Caleb had no idea what she said. "I told him to go back to the hotel or find his mahout," she said when she'd finished talking.

Steve sat on his bum and lowered his head. Caleb could all but hear Malee's tender heart breaking.

She reached a hand out and stroked the elephant's trunk. "Don't do this, okay, darling? This is hard enough as it is," she said, a sob catching her throat.

Caleb glanced up into her eyes and was stunned by the stark pain he saw there. "When we get to civilization, I'll arrange for someone to bring him to an elephant sanctuary," he said.

A tight smile lifted her lips slightly, and she turned back to continue the ascent of the mountain. Completely ignoring their repeated commands to stay, Steve trudged up the hill behind them. At least there'd be no missing the trail up to the helipad now, should they ever return.

As they exited the jungle portion of the hike, they

heard the approaching *whump, whump* of the helicopter's rotors slicing through the quiet sky.

Rescued at last.

He'd expected to feel happier.

***

Malee had never been in a helicopter before, and she clung to Caleb's hand as the machine rose into the air, its front the last bit to lift off as though giving one last kiss to the ground.

They swung away from the resort, and through the window she saw Steve sitting on his backside, staring at the machine wrenching his newfound family from him. Another piece of her heart broke off and sank into her chest. At this rate, she'd be lucky to have any of the organ survive her stay at Destiny Resort.

Should she tell Caleb her cousin owned the resort? What if he thought she'd only slept with him to try and persuade him to buy the place? Could she risk alienating her family because of her growing feelings for Caleb? Feelings she was sure he didn't return?

Yes, he'd said he wanted to continue their affair, but that was only a physical attraction. They had no real future. Whatever passion they shared wouldn't overcome the fact that he was a billionaire from the Western world and she a poor girl from a tiny village in remote Thailand.

She forced a smile and blinked away the moisture gathering behind her eyes. *Parting is such sweet sorrow* was a load of crock. It bloody well hurt like hell. And she hadn't even said goodbye yet.

The helicopter pilot had handed a manila envelope to Caleb as soon as they'd climbed in, and he was glancing through the papers inside, his mind already on his business and the life he'd had to put aside for four days. He let go of her hand as he removed some of the documents.

"Thank God," he said into the microphone attached to his headphones. His deep, rumbly voice in her ear flashed her back to his whispered words of pleasure when he'd climaxed deep inside her the first time. "Harrison has booked a suite at a luxury hotel in Chiang Mai."

"Did he say anything about your brother?"

Caleb's gaze shot to hers as though surprised by the question. He flipped another few pages. "He says Ian is still in the hospital for a few more tests, but is expected home by the weekend."

"That's good. He'll be disappointed about the resort, though. I hope it doesn't affect his health." Mentioning his brother's dreams for the hotel and its potential impact on his recovery was a low blow, but she was desperate.

"I'll be sure to break the news to him gently. I'll come up with a way to save his company. It just won't be at the hands of Destiny Resort."

"That's still a rubbish name for the place."

"You think so? The longer I stayed there, the more appropriate it seemed."

She shrugged, not sure what he could mean. If he had no intention of buying the property, what kind of destiny was it? Unless it had been one of those opposite games—

where it showed him exactly what he *didn't* want in life. Like a woman scared of her own shadow.

"Was there any response from the seller to you being stranded there?" More importantly, did he know that Bodin was the owner?

"The seller's agent apologized for the *inconvenience* and suggested we meet in Chiang Mai at my earliest availability. Are you still willing to translate?"

Was she? She'd have to declare her conflict of interest if she did. She could make up some excuse as to why she couldn't translate for him any longer. But since he was likely to tell the agent to get lost, it need never come out that the owner was her cousin.

"Sure. I may need to get a new dress, though, and some underwear." She pulled the edges of his shirt over her chest. The air conditioning inside the helicopter was waking up the girls.

"I'll buy you a new wardrobe as soon as we land. Although it will go against all my instincts to purchase lingerie for you when I prefer you without it."

Heat surged through her face. Good thing she couldn't see the pilot's face. What must he think of their conversation?

Caleb turned back to his paperwork, and she tried to concentrate on the scenery whizzing past. They flew over remote villages like the one her grandmother came from, rice fields, Buddhist monasteries, and miles and miles of jungle. Within a few days, she'd be home again. So why did she feel the same as when she'd left Thailand the first time to live with her mother in England? Like everything she knew and loved was lost to her? Another chunk of her heart fell into the void.

The helicopter touched down at Chiang Mai airport, and Caleb finally looked at his surroundings. He'd missed some of the most amazing scenery. Clearly, he'd already mentally left Thailand.

She'd barely gotten her seatbelt unbuckled when a young Thai man in a uniform bearing the logo of 137 Pillars House opened the door and helped her out of the aircraft. The hard pavement felt weird under her feet, like she'd stepped into another world.

Caleb's arm snaked around her waist, and they were ushered into the backseat of a waiting car. Bottles of ice-chilled water and champagne stood ready for them. And that was nothing on the welcome they got once they arrived at the boutique hotel. Malee doubted the Thai royal family could have been greeted more warmly.

There was no reception desk queue or forms to fill out for billionaires. They were taken directly to their suite, a private bungalow with its own swimming pool and outdoor shower screened for privacy. Malee tugged on the hem of her faded shorts and slipped off her nasty sandals the second the door was flung open. This was the kind of place Caleb had undoubtedly imagined he'd come to buy. Not the grungy Destiny Resort she'd taken him to. If she'd needed any further evidence that they were from two different worlds, this place proved it.

She wandered around the huge suite while Caleb spoke quietly with the hotel manager. There was a selection of body washes and lotions in the bathroom that smelled divine. Having washed her hair with a bar of soap for the past few days, she couldn't wait to give it a proper cleaning.

The outside door closed and seconds later, Caleb's arms pulled her against his strong, warm body. "I'm sorry to abandon you the second we arrive, but I have to make some urgent phone calls. Why don't you have a shower and relax, or make use of the spa? There should be a bathrobe for you to wear until your clothes arrive."

"What clothes?"

"The manager is arranging for a selection of items to be delivered. You'll need a dress for dinner tonight, something suitable for a business meeting tomorrow, and an outfit to travel back to your family in a few days. But take whatever you want. It's the least I can do."

Buy me some pretty things because you've enjoyed my body?

Before she could say something appropriate, he'd released her, grabbed his laptop bag, and was out the door. Fun, sexy Caleb was gone, leaving the driven businessman in charge.

Reality killed the last chunk of her heart.

Chapter Twelve

Caleb sipped his whiskey, enjoying the smooth burn as it slid down his throat. He ran a finger along his collar, but since he'd left the top two buttons undone, it wasn't his shirt that made it feel like a noose was slowly being tightened around his neck.

Business wouldn't wait, and he had to return to Canada tomorrow. And once he was back, his life would be filled with endless meetings for not one, but two companies. Exactly the kind of thing he'd been trying to escape in the first place. Getting rescued had been the stupidest thing he'd done in a long time.

His phone call to Harrison had taken so long that by the time he'd returned to the suite, Malee had gone out. It wasn't surprising, given that she'd been trapped with him for five days with only basic necessities. But when he'd called the front desk, they'd told him that she'd taken one look at the clothes they'd brought for her and gone off shopping on her own. The manager was extremely apologetic that they'd gotten the selection so wrong.

If he hadn't wanted to keep his conversation with Harrison strictly private, then he could have made his calls from the suite and reassured her. But he didn't want Malee to overhear him discussing the possibility that he'd been deliberately stranded at the resort. He'd instructed his lawyer friend to discover exactly who owned the place and demand they be at the meeting tomorrow. Caleb did not deal with middle men.

Then he'd missed her again. He was in the shower when Malee left a message that she'd meet him in the bar at seven. It was only minutes away from seven now.

His eyes scanned the crowd of almost entirely rich tourists from Europe or America. They sipped their cocktails or glasses of wine and discussed the things they'd seen that day. But what had they really experienced? Sure, they'd probably visited a few temples or gone on a sedate jungle hike. Had any of them attacked the foliage with a machete, dodged elephant droppings while lugging pails of water, or made love to a beautiful woman under a waterfall? They'd go home and declare their holiday a success without ever turning off their phones or missing an airing of the news. Just like the hundreds of vacations he'd taken before this one.

A shimmer of blue and gold caught his eye and he nearly dropped his drink. Malee approached, a vision in a traditional Thai silk dress. One shoulder and half her collarbone were bare, the other covered in a length of the material slung over her shoulder to fall behind her. A fitted skirt had a pleat in front secured by a gold belt. Her jet-black hair was once again secured in a twist at her nape, and gold sandals matched the bracelet on her upper arm. His weren't the only appreciative eyes that followed her progress across the room.

He stood as she approached and kissed her upturned cheek. "You look amazing," he said.

Her eyelids dropped briefly as though shy at his

compliment. Or maybe she was checking out his growing erection. He longed to lick his way across that exposed collarbone and up the cord at the side of her neck before plundering her mouth to see if she tasted as good as she smelled. An exotic scent, a blend of flowers and spices, subtly filled the air around her. He wasn't normally a man to show off, despite his penchant for reckless sports, but tonight he wanted everyone to know this beautiful woman was with him.

A waiter hovered discreetly beside the table as Malee sat. "What will you have to drink?" Caleb asked, shifting his chair closer to hers.

"A glass of white wine?" She looked to him for confirmation and her hesitant tone had him waving away the waiter for the moment. In putting on the traditional clothes of her country, had she suddenly remembered she was a demure Thai female? He wanted the vibrant, exciting woman he'd gotten to know over the past few days.

"What's up, Malee? Why are you second-guessing what you want all of a sudden?"

She fiddled with the pleat at the front of her dress until he stilled her hand with his. When he lifted her fingers and kissed them, she raised her eyes to his.

"This is your world, not mine. I feel out of place." Her gaze darted around the room before settling back on him.

"You don't look out of place. You own this room. And my world, as you call it, is simply a shallower reflection of yours. But if you hate it here, we'll leave immediately. I'm sure there's a backpacker hostel with a bed or two free somewhere in the city."

Her tinkle of a laugh seemed to release some of her tension. She squared her shoulders and summoned the waiter with a flick of her wrist. "I'll have white wine," she said, this time with more authority.

"Do you like champagne?" Caleb asked before the waiter could ask her what type of wine she wanted.

"I've never even tasted it."

"A bottle of Dom Pérignon, the rosé if you have it," Caleb ordered.

While the waiter went off to find the beverage, Caleb ran a finger down Malee's arm from the shoulder to her wrist, circling the gold band on her upper arm. She hauled in an unsteady breath. Room service might be a better option than eating in the restaurant.

"I'm sorry you didn't like any of the clothes that were brought to you. But this dress is stunning. Where did you get it?"

"I liked the clothes—they were just too expensive. I saw one of the tags. I could have bought a car for the cost of one outfit. So I went to visit my aunt, my father's sister. She has a boutique not too far from here and had what I needed."

"I didn't know you had family in Chiang Mai."

"Yes, Aunt Urassaya lives here. There was no work in the village, so she opened a dressmaking shop in the city a few years ago. If you want, I could introduce you. I think you'd like her, she's really nice."

His breath hitched in his throat before he could reply. "I won't have time this visit."

She nodded as though she'd already accepted the end of their affair and moved on. "Actually, I lived here in

Chiang Mai for a little bit with my parents before the accident. My father worked in one of the resorts. After he died, Mum and I moved back to Pakang Yao to live with her parents until she left for London to get work. The rest you know…" The words tumbled from her mouth. He knew her well enough now to realize she chattered when nervous.

A light shiver wracked her body, and he lifted her hand to place a kiss on the inside of her wrist. The scent of her perfume was stronger there and he couldn't help but taste her with his tongue.

Her voice was all breathy when she said, "Caleb, people are watching." She tried to pull her hand away, but he just repeated the caress. Satisfaction flowed through him when a delicate flush crept over her skin and her breathing became uneven. Definitely room service.

"I don't care. If you do, then I'll have the bar cleared so it's only us."

"You can't do that."

He raised one eyebrow. "Watch me." He was about to raise his hand to call over the resort manager, who Caleb had spied watching him from the shadows, but Malee grabbed his arm.

"No. It's fine. I'm just not used to public displays of … affection." She glanced around the room once more, but no one was paying them any attention.

Reluctantly he let go of her hand and sat back in his chair. The waiter arrived at that moment with the champagne, a bucket of ice, and two flutes. As he popped the cork, a few people looked over, obviously expecting there to be some sort of celebration or announcement at Caleb's table.

He waited until the waiter left again before raising his glass to Malee. "To our rescue," he whispered, then took her hand in his and kissed her ring finger. Let people think they were celebrating an engagement if it put Malee's sensibilities at ease. "And the time we spent together before … and after." Her eyes softened. With love? No one had ever looked at him that way before.

Dammit, he wished they were celebrating their engagement, or at least an agreement to continue their affair. He had to cement things with Malee tonight, so they didn't have to part indefinitely. Maybe she'd take up his offer to come to Canada and see the northern lights. His usual urge to move on, to avoid a relationship, had been replaced with a fierce need to hold her and keep her close for as long as he could.

Now he just had to figure out how.

***

Malee was floating on air. At first, she'd been intimidated by the evidence of Caleb's wealth. She knew he was rich, but at the resort, they'd been almost equals, both stuck in a situation where practical knowledge was worth more than money. But here, in this fabulous place, the disparity in their social statuses had hit home. The items sent over for her to try on were beautiful. But who in their right mind would pay the equivalent of a thousand pounds for one dress? Instead she'd scurried off to her aunt's shop, where the prices were reasonable and she could pay for her own clothes.

This, though, was a once-in-a-lifetime opportunity. Not to replenish her wardrobe at Caleb's expense, but to pretend, just for one night, that she was Cinderella. There'd be no happy ever after for her. But that was tomorrow's problem.

Indulging the fantasy with three glasses of champagne, she no longer cared who saw them together or what they thought. He'd suggested they have dinner in their suite, but she'd been enjoying the envious stares of the other women too much. Caleb was magnificent in his button-down shirt that enhanced the green of his eyes. His blond hair had been mussed slightly, as though he'd been running his hands through it. A pair of dark gray trousers fit him to perfection, and the silver watch he wore had caught the light on more than one occasion. No man would ever compare favorably to him. She might as well enjoy it while it lasted.

But more than his looks and obvious wealth—the possessive gleam in his eyes, the near constant touch of his hand, the sexy smile that creased his lips and released his dimple—had overwhelmed all her inhibitions. Now she was about as close to the stars as an earth-bound human could get.

"How come we're the only ones dancing?" Adele's "All I Ask" was playing through a speaker near the floor. The words were too close to their situation and sliced into her heart. So much for leaving reality until tomorrow.

As if it could slow down time, she tucked her head under his chin, her body plastered to his. It was highly inappropriate behavior in Thai culture, but at this moment, she didn't care. She'd blame her British upbringing if anyone dared mention it.

"Because I'm glaring at anyone who dares come near the dance floor," he replied, his lips grazing her temple.

"That doesn't seem fair."

"You know what they say about love and war." His hand shifted lower on her back, pressing her into his erection.

"Neither qualifies in this instance." At least, not on his part. Her last hope of stopping herself from falling in love with him had surrendered sometime between the first glass of champagne—when he'd stared into her eyes, his gaze telling her things his lips didn't dare promise—and when he'd called the manager over and told him they'd like to dance. Caleb had been attentive and, based on the blaze of lust in his eyes whenever he looked at her, quite anxious to get her alone. And naked. But he hadn't pushed or cajoled her into returning to the room, letting her set the pace for their romantic evening.

"I don't know…" His lips grazed her temple again, and his tongue darted out to taste her skin. "I want to make *love* to you, and anyone who gets in my way may well end up in a *war*."

She leaned back on his arm so she could see his face. Their gazes caught, and for what seemed an eternity, they stared into each other's eyes. Could he see the love in hers? If so, he didn't turn away in terror. "Then to avoid any unnecessary bloodshed, perhaps we should go somewhere more private."

His lips captured hers briefly. "You have a great

future as a diplomat."

But not as your girlfriend.

Before leaving, he asked the manager to send another bottle of wine and strawberries to their suite and ensure they weren't disturbed until morning.

They detoured through the gardens on the way to their bungalow.

The deep breath he pulled in before speaking warned her she wasn't going to like what he was about to say. "I have to leave tomorrow, immediately after the meeting about Destiny Resort."

Yup, that was the first chime of midnight in her Cinderella dream. Hopefully the music still playing from the restaurant masked the wail coming from her heart. "I understand. When's the meeting set for?"

"I haven't nailed down the time. It'll be confirmed in the morning." He stopped and traced the line of her lips with his thumb. "I don't want to go. Being stranded with you was the best thing that's ever happened to me."

"All good things must come to an end." She was pulling out all the trite phrases now. Next thing she'd be telling him they were never meant to be.

"Must they?" His lips replaced his finger, and his kiss swept her into a whirlwind of passion. "How about just a pause?" he asked as he finally pulled back enough to stare into her eyes. Their bodies were still pressed together, so she knew he could feel her heart hammering in her chest and the tight grip she had on his back.

"Don't do this to me, Caleb. Don't string this along. It would be better for both of us if we just say goodbye tomorrow with no false promises." It would be even better if she could let go of him, but her arms were defying her brain's order on that one.

"I live up to my promises."

"Yes. And your promise to your brother to see his company out of trouble is your first priority. Family is the most important thing. If we're not loyal to our family, how can we pledge allegiance to someone else?"

"Malee—"

"Give me a night I'll never forget, Caleb. Like Adele, that's all I ask."

He swung her into his arms. "You have the night. But this is no love song. And tomorrow I get my say."

Unless she died of pleasure.

Rather than strip off her clothes the moment the door closed behind them, Caleb examined the label on the champagne bottle, then popped the cork and poured her a glass. As he strode toward her with the bubbly in hand, his eyes caressed her body.

"Sip that while I run the bath for you," he said.

A bath? She'd showered earlier. She snagged one of the plump and delicious-looking strawberries and followed him into the bathroom, which was now lit with a hundred candles. He was pouring some heavenly scented liquid under the running water, filling the air with the misty perfume of a thousand flowers dipped in spice.

"What's with the bath? I thought we were going to have mind-blowing sex." Technically, every time they had sex, it was mind-blowing, so tonight should be no exception. With the romantic dinner, champagne, and close dancing, she was ready. She squirmed a little as he undid two of the buttons on his shirt. Make that wet and ready.

"Patience, sweetheart. A relaxing bath, a nice massage, and we'll see what happens."

She moved over to him, licked the sweet strawberry juice from her fingers, and handed him the glass of champagne. His gaze was riveted on hers as she finished unbuttoning his shirt. "Is this like some kind of date?"

"What do you mean, 'some kind of date'? This *is* a date. A very good one, I'll have you know. I took you to drinks and then dinner, I danced with you, now the bath…"

"I thought you didn't make plans. This is almost scripted." Running her hands from his ripped abs to his chest, she lightly grazed his nipples with the pad of her thumb, gratified when he hauled in a deep breath.

"According to *Cosmo* magazine, this was voted the number-one date fantasy by women under thirty."

She slid the shirt from his shoulders, taking back her wineglass so the garment could drop to the floor. He wasn't the kind of man who needed dating advice from a women's magazine. He had to be playing a game. "Number one, eh? I bet none of those women have ever lain on a hammock under the stars while being chaperoned by a four-ton elephant. Or made love behind the curtain of a waterfall." She sipped her wine as Caleb found the zipper at the back of her dress and slid it slowly down.

"Probably not," he said. "But have you ever had a bubble bath in a claw-foot tub while drinking champagne and being washed by a Canadian venture capitalist?"

"No." Her dress fell to the floor and she kicked it across the room. If things got splashy, and she sure as hell hoped they did, she didn't want the silk ruined by the water. "In the name of science, I should probably experience both and then report my findings to the fine people at *Cosmo*."

"My thoughts exactly." He took the champagne from her hand and drained the glass before giving it back to her. "Don't move."

When he returned a moment later, he was holding the bottle of champagne and the bowl of strawberries—completely naked. *Cosmo* may have been be right; this was a good fantasy.

"I like the lingerie," he said, his eyes scorching a trail over her torso. It had been her one indulgence today: the sexiest bra and panty set she could find. Considering the amount of fabric and what she'd paid, the cost per square inch rivaled that of the overpriced dress she'd been shown earlier. From the look in Caleb's eyes, however, it was worth every baht.

She ran a finger along the lace edge between her breasts. "Would you like to remove it so it doesn't get wet?"

He popped a strawberry in her mouth and filled her glass with more champagne before putting the bottle and bowl beside the tub. Then he pressed his finger along the tiny patch of fabric between her legs. "It seems I'm too late. This is already soaked."

"Doing that is not helping," she managed to say as his finger continued to torment her through the material.

"We should make the top and bottom match." He tipped her glass over her breasts, then sucked her nipples through the champagne-soaked fabric. "Good, but I prefer you without the lace filter." Releasing the hooks at the back, her bra soon fluttered out of the way. He tipped a bit more champagne over her hardened nipples and licked them again. "Much better," he said. He tugged on the side of the panties, and they gave way like an elastic left out too long in the sun. With Caleb returning to Canada tomorrow, she'd never wear them again anyway.

He lifted her into the tub and then joined her. She lay against the bath, the bubbles hiding their bodies from view. As she sipped the champagne, Caleb ran slow caresses up her legs and over her torso, stopping just before he reached her breasts. She ached for him to put his mouth on her, but he continued his feather-light touches. She was drifting again on a cloud of champagne, her body singing the tune Caleb played with such finesse.

"Caleb, please. I need you inside me," she moaned as he toyed with her clit. Their lovemaking before had always been needy and passionate. This slow, erotic buildup was torture and ecstasy at the same time.

"Not yet. Close your eyes and enjoy."

He brought her to the edge time and again, and when she thought she'd scream from frustration, he hauled himself from the bath and lifted her out. Then the drying process started. He licked the water from her body and followed with the softest towel she'd ever felt. Her knees started to give way, and she had to cling to his shoulders for support.

"Now?" Her voice begged him to take her over the edge. She reached for his erection, hoping to push him into action, but he held himself away.

"You forgot about the massage," he said, the roughness in his voice betraying his battle with self-control.

Scooping her into his arms again, he strode through to the bedroom and placed her gently on the turned-down bed. "Roll over," he commanded.

She turned on her stomach, expecting him to raise her hips and slide into her from behind, a position they both enjoyed immensely. Instead, a warm liquid drizzled over her back, and Caleb's strong yet gentle hands massaged it into her skin. It tingled, then cooled, then warmed, making every nerve ending sing the hallelujah chorus.

By the time he flipped her over and began to massage her front, she was almost mindless with pleasure. "Wait for me, babe," he said, his hot breath in her ear nearly pushing her over the edge. The ripping of the foil condom packet was the most beautiful sound she'd ever heard.

As he guided his rigid erection into her tight core, he pulled one of her nipples into his mouth with a fierce suction. She shattered into a million pieces.

All the king's horses and all the king's men would never put Malee back together again.

Chapter Thirteen

A gentle nudge pulled Caleb from dreamland into a waking fantasy. Malee leaned over him, completely naked, a look of utter bliss in her eyes. They'd made love twice more last night after the first slow, sensual time. Each kiss, each caress had driven home to him that Malee was a woman like no other and he'd be a fool to let her go.

There was a peace inside him he'd never experienced before. A sense that this was what he'd been unconsciously searching for all his life. The itch to adventure was gone. The fulfillment of just being with her was more than he'd ever imagined possible.

"Your mobile phone has been ringing repeatedly for the past twenty minutes," she said.

As if on cue, the distant ring of his cell in the other room broke through the silence.

"What time is it?"

She glanced over his shoulder to the bedside clock. "Half seven."

He didn't bother to stifle the groan that rose from his heart. The countdown to departure had begun.

"While you check your messages," Malee said as she threw back the bedsheet, "I'll be in the shower." She sauntered into the bathroom, pausing at the doorway to blow him a kiss.

With his chest feeling like Steve sat on it, Caleb exited the bed and strolled toward the sitting room, where he'd abandoned his phone and laptop yesterday. He should have shut the damn thing off. The ringing had stopped but started again before he could check his voice or email messages.

"Yes?" he answered tersely.

"Rough night?" Harrison's carefully modulated voice greeted him. His friend was a master at disguising his emotions. If Caleb had been through what Harrison had, he'd probably have locked down his feelings as well. And based on the way his body reacted to his imminent return to Canada, he might be asking for some pointers from his emotionless friend.

"Perfect night. Not sure about the day, though." Caleb ran a hand through his hair. The shower had been turned on, and he longed to join Malee. "What's up?"

"Your meeting with the resort owner is set for ten o'clock in the Kasalong Pavilion at the Four Seasons hotel. I've emailed you everything I've found on him. It seems the resort recently changed hands, but I've been unable to establish the purchase price. But I wouldn't be surprised if the amount they're asking now is wildly inflated over what they paid."

"Of that, I have no doubt."

"And I had someone go up and check on the landslide. You were right: it was deliberately set off."

The pressure in Caleb's chest increased, and he rubbed the heel of his hand against his sternum. "Interesting."

"Are you still going to buy the hotel?"

"If I can get it for the right price. It'll never work as a resort. But I might keep it as a holiday home. I've grown attached to the place."

"The place, or the woman who was trapped there with you?"

There was no point denying it. "Both."

"Well, take care, my friend. One of the key ingredients to a holiday affair is to remember that it's a holiday, not real life."

"It sure feels real."

Harrison's voice held no humor. "You want reality? The board of Doyle Destinations has called an emergency meeting. The date and time's in your calendar. And your mother's all in a flap and wants you to call."

"Transfer fifty grand into her bank account. No, wait. I'll see her first. Ask my assistant to book a time with her, and a restaurant. Actually, just get Natalie to arrange the date and time. Mother can come to my place, and I'll cook."

"You are going to cook dinner for your mother? I'm a fantastic lawyer, but I don't believe even I could get you off a murder charge if you poison her."

That startled a laugh out of Caleb. "I'm not going to poison her, at least not intentionally. I just think we need to talk, somewhere private where we can both be ourselves, with no one to overhear or judge us. Also, make sure Ian is aware of the Doyle Destinations board meeting. We'll conference him in if he's not well enough to attend in person. It's his company. He has every right to know what's going on. We'll hear what the board wants, then come up with a plan together to rescue the business."

"Wow, Thailand has really changed you," Harrison said.

"For the better, I hope."

"That remains to be seen. For all this extra work I've done, bring me a bottle of scotch from duty-free. None of that rotgut Irish whiskey you drink."

Caleb hung up with a laugh. They had an ongoing friendly feud over who made the best whiskey. Harrison had Scottish blood in his veins, so he disparaged anything not produced in his father's homeland. Whereas Caleb's Irish heritage had him supporting Irish whiskey.

Right now, though, whiskey wars weren't his focus. Caleb's attention was on joining Malee in the shower before she finished. He'd read the reports Harrison had sent later.

It was almost nine thirty by the time they'd dressed after their second shower of the morning. Things had gotten rather sticky with the leftover strawberries and champagne after the first one.

Malee emerged from the bedroom wearing a business dress and low-heeled shoes, once more the consummate professional translator.

"You could remain here at the hotel for few more days, if you like," Caleb said. "Visit with your family…"

She gave him a small smile. "No. It won't be the same without you."

He tried to swallow the lump in his throat. "I'll arrange transport for you back to your village, then."

"No need. I'm going to stay with my aunt while I apply for some jobs in Chiang Mai. If nothing comes up, I'll head back to my grandparents' village later in the week." She shrugged as if it was no big deal that they'd soon be saying goodbye … while every cell in his body rebelled at the thought.

"We need to talk, Malee."

"About the meeting?" A flicker of something passed through her eyes, but it moved too quickly for him to decipher.

"No. About us."

She glanced at her watch. "We'll have to talk on the way. You never know with the traffic here; it could take ten minutes or an hour."

He'd tried to have this conversation in the shower, but she'd distracted him. Clearly, she didn't want to discuss the future. He should leave it. Only … he couldn't. What if Malee was who he needed to endure the next six months? Would he lose his newfound center, this sense of inner peace, when he left Thailand? Left her?

The hotel's car was waiting for them when they emerged from the reception area. Malee gave the driver their destination in Thai and sat back, her eyes not meeting Caleb's.

"I have to go straight from this appointment to the airport. There's an emergency board meeting for my brother's company I need to attend."

"Then this will be our goodbye," she said. Her fingers fiddled with the handle of her bag.

"How about 'just until we see each other again'? You could come to Canada in a few weeks, and we'll see if this thing between us is going anywhere." He gently untangled her fingers from her bag and raised them to his lips.

Her gaze met his, and he read the anguish she'd tried to hide earlier. While it pained him to see her hurt, at least it meant she felt something, too. "I don't think I can do that."

"Is it the money? Because I'd send you a ticket and cover all your expenses." Even as he said it, the words came out wrong. Talk about making a woman feel bought and paid for. "I didn't mean it that way."

"I know what you meant. But it just goes to prove the huge difference between us."

"I'm a man, you're a woman. That's all the difference."

She shook her head. "Tell you what. In six weeks, if you still want me to come over, send me an email, and provided I can get away…" She pulled in an unsteady breath. "But I'm sure once you're back in Vancouver and immersed in your work, you'll soon forget me."

He put his palm against her cheek and, with his thumb, wiped away the single tear that escaped. "I'm not going to forget you." If the car hadn't pulled up in front of the Four Seasons, he'd have kissed her. But the valet opened the door, and remembering Malee's comment on the inappropriateness of PDAs in Thai culture, Caleb held back. But it didn't stop him from putting his arm around her waist as they entered the hotel.

"Mr. Doyle, we've been expecting you." The hotel manager rushed over to them when they strolled into the luxurious, air-conditioned reception area. "Is there anything I can get you? Would your wife like to have tea in our orchid nursery while you attend your meeting?"

Caleb reluctantly removed his hand from Malee and shook the hotel manager's. "This is Ms. Wattana, my translator."

"Sawatdee-kah," Malee said as she put her palms together and bowed. Thankfully, the surprise was carefully masked on the hotel manager's face by the time she straightened. "Has the other party arrived for our meeting?" she asked.

There was a flush to her skin. Was she embarrassed to be mistaken for his wife, or was her high color because he'd had his hand on her body when he'd introduced her?

"Yes, please come this way." The manager led them through the hotel to a small, private building at the edge of the rice terrace. He knocked once on the ornately carved wooden door and flung it open.

The two men at the table stood, the heavy chairs scraping against the wooden floor as they rose.

Caleb blinked, sure he was seeing things. He turned to Malee. The color that had earlier suffused her cheeks drained away.

"Malee? What the hell is your cousin doing here?"

Then it hit him. All the blood squeezed from his heart. It had all been a grand set-up. Him being stranded at the resort had clearly been prearranged. But how much of Malee's performance was genuine? Or had it all been staged to get him emotionally invested in the place? No wonder she hadn't wanted to commit to coming to Canada. If he hadn't insisted that the owner attend this meeting, he'd have been none the wiser. *Family is the most important thing. If we're not loyal to our family, how can we pledge allegiance to someone else?* Her words rang in his mind.

He'd been played to perfection.

***

Malee forced down the panic that threatened to overwhelm her. Caleb's body was rigid, fury blazing in his eyes. And when his gaze met hers, the tenderness she normally saw had been replaced by disgust. His lips curled in a sneer as he stepped further into the room, waiting for the hotel manager to close the door behind them.

"Keeping it all in the family, I see," he said.

"Caleb, I—"

He held his hand up, his Adam's apple bobbing as he swallowed. "You are here to translate. That is all."

Her internal organs decided to rearrange themselves inside her. She'd been put in her place as succinctly as if he'd slapped her.

"Mr. Doyle," Bodin said, while Malee translated. "If you will please sit, I can explain."

"I don't need an explanation. You trapped me at the resort—"

"What do you mean, *trapped*? The landslide was an accident, a result of the monsoon," Malee said. She put her hand on his arm but snatched it back when his eyes blazed with anger.

"No, it wasn't. We were deliberately stranded." Caleb

turned back to Bodin. "You clearly instructed your cousin to convince me to purchase the place. She did an amazing job; I was prepared to make you an offer."

Malee relayed the statement in Thai, and her stupid cousin had a huge grin on his face. Didn't he realize how this looked to Caleb? Bodin might not know that Malee had slept with Caleb, but he must have twigged that something was going on between them.

"I'm pleased to hear it." Bodin resumed his seat as though he expected negotiations to proceed.

"You mistake me. My only reason to purchase the resort was to be near Malee. However, as I now see her treachery in this matter, I no longer desire to be close to her. I will begin legal proceedings as soon as I return to Canada to reclaim the deposit my brother paid, as well as compensation for the five days you, in effect, held me hostage."

As Malee translated, her voice shaking with the effort to keep from sobbing her heartbreak, the blood drained from her cousin's face.

Caleb waited until she'd finished speaking before he turned to her. "You were right about one thing—this is our goodbye."

She wanted to argue with him, make him listen. She was desperate to tell him she'd just found out Bodin was the owner yesterday, that she hadn't meant to deceive him, that she'd had nothing to do with the landslide. But with the other men present, it wasn't something she could do. Instead, she bowed her head and waited until the door slammed behind him.

Goodbye, Caleb. Her chest ached like her heart had

been ripped from it, still beating.

The man who had been sitting beside Bodin also stood. Malee assumed he was the agent who had been dealing with the initial negotiations, however her cousin didn't bother to introduce her. After he, too, left, she turned to Bodin.

"You could have warned me you would be here," she said.

"It wouldn't have mattered if you'd have done what I asked you," he said.

She should have let it go. Her cousin faced the loss of everything. But only because he'd been greedy. And the ultimate price had been her heart.

"No. You should never have put me in that position. And you damn well should never have stranded us at the resort."

Bodin's eyes were wide, his mouth open, as though the teddy bear he'd grown up with had suddenly started spouting obscenities at him. Well, she was done with being a good girl.

"I did it for the family, Malee. One look at the place wouldn't be enough. He had to stay long enough to fall in love."

"With the hotel or me?"

"Either would have done."

"And did you never think that maybe I'd become emotionally involved and have my heart broken?"

Bodin's laugh grated against her agony. "Then you're a silly girl. Did you think it was going to be like one of those romance novels you love to read? Was the big-shot billionaire supposed to fall for the child afraid of the dark?"

With two steps, she was in front of him. Her slap across his cheek sounded through the room like a crack of thunder. "I finally met a man who treated me with respect. I'll no longer allow you talk to me this way."

Swiveling on her heel, she strode from the room, hoping to make it into a taxi before the tears fell. She would not cry in front of Bodin. But that didn't mean the waterworks would hold off indefinitely.

Caleb hadn't even given her a chance to defend herself. He'd damned her with her cousin. He obviously didn't love her, or even think enough of her, to listen to her side of the story. She'd been well and truly dissed by both men. But only one of them mattered.

Chapter Fourteen

"Sawatdee-kah," Malee called without looking up as the bell above her aunt's shop door tinkled, alerting her to the arrival of a new customer. She finished wrapping a ribbon around a box, then glanced at the woman who'd walked into the tiny store. She blinked twice before her brain agreed with her eyes.

"Mum! Why didn't you tell me you were coming? I'd have met you at the airport."

"I wanted to surprise you. Besides, until I got on the plane, I wasn't sure I was coming. It was a last-minute decision."

Malee enveloped her mother in a hug. It was the first embrace she'd had in six weeks—since Caleb had accused her of deception and dropped her like a flaming satay. But as her mother was five centimeters shorter than Malee, it didn't have the same effect as being snuggled against a broad, muscled, Canadian chest.

"Is everything okay?" She searched her mother's face, trying to detect if the unexpected visit was the result of some tragedy. Instead of distress, her mother almost glowed with happiness.

"It's all good. No, better than that. Everything is fantastic. There's someone I want you to meet."

Oh, God. If her mother had brought some potential boyfriend for her, she'd fall apart. She hadn't told anyone what had happened with Caleb. And given the silence from the rest of her family, she assumed Bodin hadn't blabbed either. But maybe Gran had sensed something was amiss when Malee had phoned to say she wouldn't be returning right away. Then her grandparent must have called her mother…

Malee glanced behind her parent, then to the pavement outside the shop, searching for whomever she'd brought with her. No one lingered, waiting for an introduction. "Who?"

"Howard, my fiancé." Her mother flashed a small diamond solitaire in front of Malee's face. The gem reflected the love and hope in her mother's eyes.

"What?" Too many sleepless nights had Malee's brain on permanent holiday. Her mother hadn't mentioned any love interest in the past couple of months.

"His name is Howard Williams, and he's the pastry chef at the Lancaster."

"But Mum, you never said a word about him in any of your letters, or even mentioned him before I left." Malee sank into the chair they kept for people who were waiting for a fitting.

"Well, we never actually had a date until you left. We mostly just chatted at work. And you were getting over your break-up with your boyfriend, so I didn't want to flaunt my relationship in your face." Her mother sank to her knees in front of Malee. "Please, sweetie, I hope you can be happy for me."

"Of course, I'm happy for you." She hugged her mother again. "It's just such a shock. I thought you wanted to return to Thailand. I'd envisioned us all living together again: you, me, Yai and Pu… I wanted us to be a family."

"We can't go back to what was, Malee-*ya*. And we'll always be family. But I deserve to have my own life, and you do, too. And unless my mother-eyes deceive me, you're not happy here, either. Come back to London. Howard said he wouldn't mind if you lived with us for a while."

Malee was already shaking her head before her mother finished speaking. She'd been a third wheel in her grandparents' house. No way was she going to be one with her mother and her step-dad-to-be.

Her last dreams went down the drain like a monsoon rain. And even those had dried up in the past couple of weeks. The few storms she'd had to endure without Caleb had been doubly bad. Not only had she had her fears to deal with, but also the remembrance of all she'd lost.

"I don't fit in in London," she said. "I thought I'd feel more at home here, but that hasn't happened, either."

"Because home is where your heart is, not a physical location on the planet. Find a good man to love, and wherever he is, that's where you'll belong."

Malee burst into tears and was once again enveloped in her mother's arms. "Oh, Mum, I found where I belong, but now I'm barred from going there."

As she explained to her mother what had happened, omitting some of the more personal details, anger radiated from her parent.

"Just wait until I speak with Bodin. He had no right to put you in that position."

"It doesn't matter, Mum. What's done is done. There's no point putting the family through any more strife."

"But if Bodin called the man and explained…"

Malee squeezed her eyes tightly closed to stop another round of tears. She'd already gone over every possible scenario in her mind. Bodin calling… Calling Caleb herself… Showing up at his office… Even if he listened to her, it didn't change the bottom line. They'd had a holiday affair. The holiday was over. It was time she moved on with her life.

"It wouldn't make a difference. And we were far too different for the relationship to last anyway." *I'm a man, you're a woman. That's all the difference.* If only Caleb's words didn't keep repeating in her mind.

"Differences are what make a relationship interesting. If you marry someone just like yourself, you'll be bored in days. What's so different about this man that you think you won't last?"

"He's an adrenaline junkie. No offense, Mum, but I don't want to end up like you, widowed early with a small child to care for. If Papa hadn't been reckless, driving crazy and getting killed, then you wouldn't have had to go to London to get work and we could have all stayed together and been a family."

"Malee, there are no guarantees in life or love. Your father's passion and enthusiasm were what drew me to him in the first place. He had courage to do the things I never dreamed of, and with his help, I overcame a lot of my own insecurities. I would never have had the guts to go to London and apply for a job in a top-end restaurant if it hadn't been for his faith in me."

"But your marriage was so short. Wouldn't you have preferred it if he was a little less reckless and you'd lived happily ever after together?"

"Yes, perhaps. But even if I knew we'd only have nine years together, I'd have taken that over a lifetime with a different man. I loved him, and I wouldn't have given up the time we had for anything. Especially because that relationship gave me you."

"And is your new fiancé reckless as well?"

"No. Howard is sweet and caring and exactly what I need in my life now. But tell me about your Caleb. Does he make you feel special?"

"Yes. He even thinks my phobias are reasonable. And when he holds me in his arms, I'm not afraid anymore."

"He sounds like just the man for you."

Except he was gone for good. Nothing could stop the tears now.

***

Sunshine glistened on the fresh snowfall, making it seem as though he could reach out and touch the mountains across the inlet. A seaplane took off from the harbor, banked left, and headed toward Victoria. From his office window on the thirty-third floor, Caleb could see dozens of office workers scurrying along the sidewalks, running errands or just out for some exercise on their lunch breaks. Vancouver was at its most beautiful. Still, he longed for the rich greens of the jungle tapestry, the pounding of the rain on the roof, and the smell of tropical flowers and lemongrass.

A knock sounded on his door and he called out, "Enter," without even bothering to turn around to see who it was. He knew it wasn't the person he wanted to see, that was for damn sure. What was Malee doing now? Has she returned to her village, or was she still in Chiang Mai? Did she take cold showers like he did, reliving their times in the waterfall together, the icy water stinging the skin but oddly adding to the pleasure of her touch?

"Caleb?"

He turned at the concern in his assistant's voice.

"Yes, Natalie?"

"Are you … okay?"

"Of course, why wouldn't I be?"

"Because I've been standing here for two minutes talking to you and you haven't answered my questions."

"Sorry. I've got a lot on my mind. What did you ask?"

"I said that with the threat of more snow, your afternoon meetings have canceled. So your schedule is now clear. Do you want to go through the property audit report for Doyle Destinations? Or are you going to take advantage of the fresh powder, grab your snowboard, and bag a few runs?" Natalie's smile told him which option she thought he'd go for. And two months ago, it would have been as simple as that. Today, his heart just wasn't into it.

"Bring through the audit report. But why don't you head home and start the weekend early?"

"Are you sure?" The note of hope in her voice was tempered by professionalism. Natalie had been his assistant for five years, and since his return from Thailand, she'd put in almost as many late nights as he had. Sleeping hadn't been an option for him, so he'd worked as much as possible. His staff had had to cope with his insane hours and mixed productivity.

The only night Natalie got home on time was when Caleb met his mother for dinner once a week. Evidently Claire Doyle hated awkward silences almost as much as Malee did, and slowly, he'd been able to learn about the woman behind the cold façade.

He'd never in a million years have guessed that his mother had been part of a punk rock band in high school. In fact, he hadn't believed her until she'd produced a photo. Nor had he known that she had a weakness for Purdy's chocolate Hedgehogs but had to eat them back-first so they couldn't *see* what was coming. He now had a standing order for the confections to be delivered every Monday.

Another couple of months of mother-son date nights and he might even get up the courage to ask her why she'd married his father. He'd avoided it so far, just in case she had once loved his dad. At the moment, he couldn't deal with hearing about another love affair gone bad.

God, it had been almost two months since he'd left Thailand. When would he get over Malee? When would he stop listening for her cooking in the kitchen whenever he returned home? When would he not roll over and want to snuggle against her warmth for five more minutes in the morning?

Nathalie was staring at him like he'd lost his mind

again. Which, technically, he probably had. "Absolutely. Have a good weekend."

The door had barely closed behind her when it swung open again. This time, Harrison stood in the doorway, a bottle of scotch and two glasses in hand. "We need to talk."

Caleb slumped into one of the visitor chairs in front of his desk. "Are you breaking up with me?"

"If I was, I wouldn't be sharing the best whisky with you." Harrison sat in the chair next to Caleb's and poured them both a generous drink.

"*Sláinte.*"

"*Slaandjivaa,*" Harrison replied, knocking his glass against Caleb's before taking a swig.

The scotch was excellent, but it would be a colder day than this before Caleb would admit as much. "What do we need to talk about? You not enjoying being Partner? Want to rename the firm Mackenzie and Doyle?"

"Nope, not that. I'm loving it. And we'll revisit the name change at a later date. I want to talk to you about Thailand."

Caleb took a hefty swallow and sat up straighter. "What's there to say? The resort wasn't right, so I didn't buy it."

"And the woman?"

Caleb drained the glass. "She wasn't right, either." The burn in his chest could have been either the whisky or the mention of Malee's betrayal—it was hard to tell at this point.

Harrison refilled Caleb's glass. "If I knew you were going to swig the stuff, I'd have brought a cheaper bottle."

In deference to the quality of the amber nectar, Caleb sipped this time. "You seriously came to my office to talk about a woman? Sounds like you need one."

This time, it was Harrison who took a large gulp. "No way. Not going there again. But you seem to have been skewered by Cupid's poison dart. You're moodier than a bear woken up mid-hibernation."

"I've got a lot on my desk."

"Ha. You thrive on pressure. You handled the Doyle Destinations board like they were a bunch of kindergartners and you held the jar of chocolate chip cookies."

The first genuine smile in a long time creased Caleb's lips. "They did roll over rather easily." With a not-so-small cash injection from himself, and the promise of an inventory overhaul, the board had unanimously endorsed Caleb as interim CEO while his brother Ian recovered from his heart attack.

Another change following his return was that he also now met weekly with his brother. They discussed the future of Doyle Destinations and Ian's vision for the company and the way to achieve that. And surprisingly, rather than reject Caleb's suggestions outright, Ian now listened and agreed, with a few insightful additions from having lived in the industry for the last two decades. Even more amazing, Ian had even made Caleb laugh a time or two when he'd impersonated the way their long-gone father would have reacted to the corporate overhaul. Oddly enough, those were the times Caleb missed Malee the most. He couldn't help wanting to share these newfound family insights with her.

Harrison put down his glass on the desk heavily, as though aware that Caleb's thoughts had drifted once more back to Thailand and he wanted not-so-subtly to remind him of his presence. "Tell me about Malee." His best friend disappeared behind the guise of a seasoned prosecution lawyer.

Caleb sipped the whisky for a minute, buying time and allowing the spirit to dull the agony that threatened to consume him whenever her name was mentioned. "There's nothing to tell. We had an affair while we were stranded. Then I discovered that it was her cousin who owned the resort and she'd been playing me all along."

"Had she? Did she know her cousin owned the resort?"

A chill crept across his skin. How many sleepless nights had he asked himself that same question? "I assume so. They're a close family. How could she not know?"

"In other words, you're not one-hundred-percent positive she knew."

"No."

"But she'd deceived you all along as to why you should buy the resort?"

"Not really. She said it was to help the local economy and so her mother, who is a professional chef, could return to live near her elderly parents."

"My God, this Malee sounds like a real piece of work. Imagine wanting to help her mother and neighbors. Looks like you had a lucky escape. Who would want to be with a woman who cares for other people like that?"

"Shut up, Harrison."

"Still, she knew the resort was in a terrible state. You must have been angry when she led you all the way there under a false impression."

"Actually, she told me it had been abandoned and was near ruin when I met her at the airport." Why would she have done that if she'd known her cousin owned the place and intended to strand them there? Icicles inched down his spine now. He thought it might snow in the room before Harrison was finished grilling him. He sipped more of the whisky to try and warm himself.

"Dastardly. Honest and helpful. Tell me some more about the terrible things she did."

"She adopted a stray elephant and called him Steve."

Not even Harrison could hide a smile at that revelation. "Unbelievable. And I bet she used all the hot water before you got any."

"Actually, there was no hot water. We had to shower in the nearby waterfall." The whisky wasn't needed now, as heat flooded his body when he remembered the taste of Malee's rock-hard nipples. The caress of her hands on his body, the way she'd drop little kisses on his chest as they both floated back to earth after a climax.

Harrison's voice was an unwanted intrusion on his memories. "And once you realized you were stranded, she probably sat around and bitched the whole time, making you do all the work to keep the two of you fed and safe."

"No, she did all of the cooking. She's amazing, making a tasty meal out of nothing. And she cleaned and showed me some amazing sights…" His heart rate slowed just remembering the mist hanging over the valley, caressing the sides of the mountains. His center aligned once more before going off-kilter again. The itch to move, to do something, just so he could feel alive consumed him. But every dangerous activity he considered held no appeal. The only thing he wanted, the only thing that would help, was eleven thousand kilometers away.

"I have one more question," Harrison said after a minute.

Caleb pulled his gaze from his glass to focus on his friend. "And that is?"

"What the hell are you doing, sitting here with me, when you could be with her?"

Like he hadn't been asking himself the same question for the past ten minutes.

Knowing when he'd won an argument, Harrison grabbed his bottle of scotch and stood, turning before he exited the room to launch his final volley. "When you get back, we can discuss changing the firm name to Mackenzie Investments. I seem to have all the good ideas around here."

Caleb threw a wadded-up ball of paper at his friend, although he couldn't deny the accusation.

It was time to go get his woman. Or die trying.

Chapter Fifteen

"Bodin, I'm absolutely going to kill you this time if you don't slow down," Malee said as the Jeep returned to all four wheels after taking the corner on two.

Her cousin glanced over, then lifted his foot off the accelerator. "Sorry. Just want to make sure you make it to the airport early enough this time."

"I'll settle for getting there alive. Now, you swear this buyer knows you own the resort and that I'm your cousin? He's not worried about a conflict of interest on my part?"

"I disclosed everything. And you'll be arriving and leaving by helicopter, so there's no chance you'll be stranded."

She just nodded, not yet able to think about her time with Caleb without searing pain.

"If we're going by helicopter, why didn't I just meet the buyer at the hotel's helipad? Why drive all the way to Nan?" The road to the resort had almost been repaired, a new bridge structure put in over the washed-out part. It wasn't open to vehicular traffic yet, but she could have walked across.

"He wants an aerial view of the hotel first with someone who knows the area."

"Are you coming with us? What do I need to translate if you're not there?"

"Enough questions, Malee. Just go with Mr. Mackenzie to the resort, show him around, and I'll meet you back in Nan in a few hours. If he's interested, we'll conclude negotiations. If not, you're still getting paid for a day's guiding and translating."

"I can't believe I'm doing this again after last time," she said, more to herself than her cousin. It had taken Bodin three days to convince her to accept this job. Only by begging and getting her grandmother on the phone had she even agreed to listen to his proposal. He'd promised that everything was above board. But before she even set foot in the helicopter, she was going to make sure this Mr. Mackenzie knew the hotel was in rough shape and that she was related to the owner.

"I know I screwed up, cousin. I can't tell you how sorry I am. You're a better person than me to forgive me like this."

Now she knew they'd already crashed, she had a head injury, and was imaging this. A contrite Bodin didn't exist in real life.

Except the diesel fumes belching from the bus in front of them and the roar of the jet landing as they arrived at the airport were too strong to be her imagination. There was no point changing into the dress and heeled shoes tucked into her bag. If they were hiking from the helipad down to the resort, she'd need to be in shorts, T-shirt, and boots. She'd only brought the outfit because Bodin insisted she have something to change into in case the place sold and they went for a celebratory dinner. Why she couldn't just leave it with him, she had no idea.

If nothing else, she'd at least get to see if Steve was

still there and okay. Had Caleb lived up to his promise to get the animal into a sanctuary? Or after the way they'd ended things, had he turned his back on all things Thai?

"How am I supposed to recognize this guy?"

"I made you a sign." Bodin handed her a piece of cardboard with *Mackenzie* written in Thai script. So not helpful. "Meet you back here in a few hours," he said with a wave.

The airport at Nan looked the same as it had two months ago. This time, she was different. The excited young woman who loved romance novels and wanted the resort up and running had had her dreams obliterated under the stiletto heel of reality. And even if the hotel did sell to this buyer, she could never work there. Too many memories of Caleb resided in the resort.

And having met her mother's fiancé, who was as sweet and supportive as advertised, Malee knew there was no chance of the family being reunited. The six-week mark, when she'd suggested Caleb contact her, had passed without a word. She'd finally convinced her stupid heart that it was over. Now, if only it would get on with healing.

At least she had an interview scheduled with the British embassy in Bangkok next week. Her dual citizenship and fluency in both English and Thai would hopefully get her at least an entry-level job. As for her dislike of living in a major city, well, she'd just have to suck it up. Not everyone got what they wanted in life.

Thankfully, the woman at the car rental desk didn't remember Malee from the last time, and she was able to borrow a marker to write Mr. Mackenzie's name on the cardboard in English.

She'd just handed the marker back to the woman when a deep, Canadian-accented voice behind her said, "I believe you're here to meet me."

No! She had to be upside down at the bottom of a ravine. Caleb couldn't be here. He'd walked away from her, and Thailand, without a word or backward glance.

She hauled in a deep breath and turned. Might as well play this last-breath fantasy to the end. "Actually, I'm here to meet Mr. Mackenzie. Your translator doesn't seem to have arrived yet." There, that sounded like a woman who wasn't delusional.

"Once again, I'm stepping in. Mr. Mackenzie was suddenly taken ill. Something about some bad scotch he had. Anyway, he asked me to come in his place."

She reached out a hand to touch his face, run a finger over his beautiful lips to make sure he was real. And if he wasn't? No way was she going to end this dream so soon.

But neither was she going to be a pushover. Not anymore. "You've already seen the resort and rejected it."

"I believe I may have been over-hasty in my earlier decision."

She shook her head. This couldn't be happening. "Caleb, what the hell are you doing here?"

He took both her hands in his, and her heart began to fibrillate. "I've come to beg your forgiveness and ask if there's any way we can start again."

"Start again?" For a woman who was fluent in four

languages, words were clearly not her friend at the moment.

A cheeky grin lifted Caleb's lips, revealing the dimple she couldn't resist. "Well, maybe not right from the very beginning. I thought perhaps we could pick up where we left off the last time we were at the waterfall near Destiny Resort."

Heat swept through her. Was it the last flush of warmth before she died? Before she said something stupid, she had to know if this was real. "You have to pinch me to make sure I'm not dreaming."

"How about I kiss you instead?" He let go of her hands and in one flawless move had his arms around waist and his lips on hers. How it was possible to convey tenderness and regret in a kiss, Malee didn't know. But Caleb managed it.

When he finally released her, the woman at the rental desk sighed. Malee had forgotten they had an audience. "This is all well and good, Caleb. But it doesn't erase the fact that we are still from two different worlds."

He took her hand in his and gently tugged her toward the door to the helipad. "Sometimes worlds collide and create something new. Come back to the resort with me, if only for a few hours. I want to show you my vision for our life together. Then we can work out a compromise or… No, I'm not going to end that sentence. Because I can't think of letting you go again now that I've had you in my arms once more."

She couldn't think how they were going to stay together. But at least they'd have a proper goodbye this time. He helped her into the waiting helicopter, and within minutes, they were airborne. She squeezed his hand tightly until the machine reached a level flight path. Even after that was achieved, he didn't let her go.

"Does Bodin know it's you coming to see the resort?" she asked as they left Nan behind and flew over dense jungle. As much as she was still annoyed with her cousin, she'd hate to see his hopes and dreams dashed again. The extended family had gotten together, pooled their money, and made a few mortgage payments on the place to buy him a little more time.

"Yes. And we've already negotiated a tentative deal, depending on how our conversation goes today."

She slipped her hand out of his. "That's not fair. If I say no to you, the deal falls apart, and my cousin, stupid and greedy as he is, loses his business. You're using my love for my family as leverage to get what you want."

"Never. I have agreed to purchase the property no matter what happens with us. The only question is what I will use it for."

She tilted her head to the side. "What are the options?"

"Patience, sweetheart. We'll discuss them when we get there."

It didn't take long before they approached the landing area near the resort. There were tarps strewn about. "What's this?"

"I've had elephant food dropped here every few days. It's easier for the helicopter if they drop it on a tarp. Then every two weeks, they land and collect the used tarps."

"You've been feeding Steve since we left?"

"Yes. I called a couple of sanctuaries, but they were

either full or considered it too risky to add a bull elephant to their existing populations. They advised that the best thing for him would be to just leave him here and assist with food now and again."

"That must be costing you a fortune."

"It's only money." Said someone who had a lot. But beneath the nonchalance was a heart of pure gold.

The helicopter landed, but took off again as soon as she and Caleb were a respectable distance away. The wind kicked up by the rotors blew her hair in her face and made talking impossible.

"Don't worry, it will come back in three hours," Caleb said as soon he could talk without shouting.

She crossed her arms over her chest. "And what are we going to do for three hours?"

"Did I mention the waterfall?" His cheeky smile and the re-emergence of the damned dimple weakened her knees but not her resolve.

"Caleb, I'm not having sex with you. You walked away from me without even giving me the chance to explain. Worse, you didn't trust me. Do you know how much that hurt?" The chopper must have blown some dust in her eye, because tears trickled down her face.

He wiped the wetness from her cheeks with his thumbs. "I know. I was an idiot. Will you come down to the resort and let me explain?"

Having just accused him of not listening to her, she couldn't very well do the same to him. "All right."

The path down to the hotel was now well trampled by Steve and a fairly easy descent. That didn't stop Caleb from taking her hand and even wrapping his arm around her waist at times. Typically, her body turned traitor and reacted to his nearness. Her nipples pebbled as though advertising their need to be touched, and the dampness between her thighs betrayed her arousal.

At this rate, they'd be lucky to make it to the hotel before ripping their clothes off and shocking Steve.

Only the elephant wasn't the one surprised when they reached the back of the hotel. The place had been transformed.

What did Caleb have in mind?

***

After a quick glance around the exterior of the resort, Caleb's eyes never wavered from Malee's face. It had taken every ounce of self-control not to deepen that kiss at the airport, find the nearest empty room, and show her exactly how much he'd missed her. Even now, standing a meter apart, his body swayed toward hers.

If she rejected his proposal… No, he couldn't go there, couldn't contemplate the rest of his life without her. But did he dare ask her to give up her home, her family, to come live with him? Because in every scenario he'd tried, he could neither walk away from his businesses nor run them from a remote mountain village in northern Thailand.

"It looks amazing. How did you…? Why did you…?"

"I flew in a bunch of people last week after I closed the deal with your cousin. And the reason is you. I wanted it to live up to your vision for the place. Did I get it close?"

"It's so beautiful. Even better than when it was first built."

He forced his gaze from Malee to take in the surroundings once more. The gardens and yard had been transformed, replanted with tropical flowers and shrubs—the red, pink, and cream flowers that reminded him of Hawaii and the white flowers that smelled like Malee. The herb garden had been cleared and restocked. A new coat of white paint made the resort gleam in the sunshine. No more vines wrangled their way onto balconies. And a brand-new, cozy patio set sat on the terrace where they'd eaten their meals.

"Are you going to open it as a retreat for stressed-out executives?" She'd taken a few steps closer to him, and the subtle scent of flowers and lemongrass came with her.

"If that's what you want. Or … it could be a family home." He held his breath.

"A family home? It's kind of big. You could fit half the village in here."

He shrugged. "I like space. And privacy."

"You're going to live here?"

"Part time. But only if you're here with me."

"Caleb…"

Hope flared briefly in her eyes before they became clouded with doubt once more.

"Hear me out, okay?" he asked.

She nodded and didn't resist when he took her hand and led her over to the terrace. So far, there was no sign of Steve. He was undoubtedly waiting in the forest for Caleb to attempt a kiss.

He sank onto the love seat and released a silent sigh as Malee sat next to him. His arm automatically came around her shoulders, and she snuggled against his chest. The breath he drew in came so much easier.

"Up until two months ago, I've lived on the surface of emotion. Me, my parents, my brother—we were all wrapped up in their own lives. We were a family in name only. I didn't do the typical rebellion thing, trying to get their attention. I was happy to go my own way, make my own rules, and live my life pleasing myself.

"The few times my mother showed some concern about my welfare, she wanted something. After Dad passed and Ian's company became less profitable, I was the source of additional income for her. Every phone call, every sudden appearance at my door, ended with a request for something. I equated displays of affection with ulterior motives."

"It's not like that with me," she whispered.

"I know. But when I discovered that it was your cousin who owned the resort, I immediately went to what I knew. I thought all the tenderness you'd shown me, your concern when I climbed the rock face by the waterfall, were because you wanted me to buy the hotel and help your family."

She was shaking her head before he'd even finished. "I only found out Bodin owned the resort the day we were rescued. I wanted to tell you ... but you said you'd never buy it, so it didn't seem to matter. What hurt the most was that you didn't even give me a chance to explain."

"Because I was afraid you'd confirm my suspicion.

You see, by then I'd realized that I was falling in love with you. I was terrified I'd hear the words 'I played you' come from the lips I wanted to kiss for the rest of my life."

Malee pulled away from him and for a second, his heart stalled. Then she straddled him and put both hands on his face. "You were falling in love with me?"

"I've fallen. Completely. Utterly. Irrevocably. I love you, Malee Wattana."

"I love you, too." She sat back on his thighs, a beautiful, mischievous smile curving her lips. "And you want to live here with me?"

His heart thrilled to hear she returned his love. And while he hated to dim the light in her eyes, he had to be honest with her. "I can't live here full time. I have my own business to run, as well as my brother's for the time being. And as much as I love it here, and you, I need to keep busy. I thought this could be a place I come to when I need to get away, recharge, recalibrate."

"And would I stay here while you go back to Canada?"

"No. I can't sleep without you next to me. Please, will you consider moving to Vancouver? It's much nicer than London. It's on the ocean, and the mountains are right there so you don't feel hemmed in by buildings. I have a penthouse condo with an amazing view. But we can get a house out in the countryside if that would make you feel better. And a cottage by a lake for weekend getaways. And of course—"

She put her lips on his, effectively silencing him. The pure love in her kiss stole his breath but oddly sapped the rest of the tension from him.

"If you are in any of those places, I'll be happy," she said when eventually she ended the embrace. "I've learned some hard truths in the past two months as well."

"Such as?"

"That the dream life I imagined here was an empty illusion. I thought that if my mother came home, I'd have a family again, like before my dad died. But my mum actually wants to live in London. She's fallen in love with someone there, so won't be coming back to Thailand. Plus, my grandparents don't really need me. Not yet anyway. They like having the house to themselves."

A faint blush stained her cheeks. Had she walked in on another amorous encounter between her grandparents? He hoped he and Malee would still be enjoying each other well into their sunset years.

"So what do you want? Where do you see your life?"

"Somewhere with you. I want to make my own family, with a husband and eventually children. I can't recreate what was, but I can make something new."

Their kiss was interrupted by a loud elephant blast a few meters away.

"Looks like our chaperone is back," he said against her lips.

"Just in time. I was about to rip your clothes off." She undid a couple of buttons on his shirt and slid her hand over his pounding heart.

"Damn elephant and his timing."

Malee's laugh bounced off the hotel and disappeared into the jungle. "We'll have lots of time for love. We still need to talk. As much as I love you, there are a few things we must negotiate, and not just where we'll live."

His nod became a groan as her hands slipped further under his shirt and traced the ridges of his abdomen. "I'm not going to ask you to marry me just yet, Malee. Because we've only spent a week together, and I need you to be one-hundred-percent sure about our love when I pop the question. But know this: I love you and I want to spend the rest of my life with you, wherever that may take us in this world. I will spend each day trying to make you happy. I will be your shelter during every thunderstorm, and your light when it gets dark."

She leaned forward again as though about to kiss him, then pulled back. "What about your adventuring? It will kill me a little more each time you risk your life. I don't want to change you, Caleb. I love you. But I'm not sure I can survive the constant worry."

He closed his eyes for a second and tried to imagine his life without adventure sports. A faint twinge struck his heart. Then he tried to imagine his life without Malee and the whole organ threatened to seize up.

"You will be my greatest adventure. I promise not to do anything that scares you too much. No more bouldering. I'll use ropes and anchors in the future. Will that help?"

"Maybe if you taught me to rock climb, I wouldn't be so scared."

"I thought you had a fear of heights."

"Well, my fear of thunderstorms disappears when I'm in your arms, so hopefully my fear of heights will diminish if you're right behind me. In any event, I'd like to try something that means so much to you."

"Then that's a definite yes. You know I'd never let you fall."

"Except further in love with you."

"That, babe, is going to be my ongoing mission."

This time when they kissed, Steve let out a loud huff and sat on his backside at the edge of the terrace.

"Get used to it, friend," Caleb said. "'Cause there's going to be a lot of this and probably more from now on."

Steve closed his eyes and then put his trunk over them. Malee laughed so hard she almost fell off Caleb's lap.

"Just my luck to be stuck with the world's most dramatic elephant," he said as his hands slid under Malee's T-shirt to caress her breasts through the lace of her bra. He caught her moan of pleasure in another blistering kiss. Much more of this and they'd be headed to the waterfall.

"Somehow, I feel your luck is about to get better." She pulled off her T-shirt, and her bra soon joined it on a patio chair nearby.

No way was he giving Steve the opportunity to interfere. He stood so she straddled his waist. The seam of her shorts pressed against his rock-hard erection. As he strode toward the hotel, he prayed the spider that had originally lived in the front area had permanently relocated, because the reception desk was as far as they were going to get. But man, what a welcome.

He'd finally found home.

Epilogue

Malee gave herself a moment just to stare. It was the same every time she saw Caleb. Her heart sped up, her mouth went dry, her knees trembled slightly, and she had the urge to throw herself at him. She'd figured living together would have cured her of at least some of these symptoms, but they'd only gotten stronger.

Today, he would become her husband. Her hand flitted to her still-flat stomach. In about seven months, they would welcome a baby, and two would become three. Four, if she counted Steve.

They hadn't planned to have a child so soon. But one reckless night as they celebrated their engagement and christened their new cottage on Pitt Lake had resulted in an unplanned but not unwelcome pregnancy. So the wedding date had been moved forward. Not that she minded.

Harrison, the best man, waited downstairs next to a healthier Ian, the other groomsman. Sarah, Ian's wife, had quickly become one of Malee's favorite people and had agreed to be her matron of honor. In Vancouver, they all met at least once a month for a family dinner with Caleb's mother who, according to her soon-to-be-husband, was slowly melting.

Malee still found Claire rather stiff and formal, but she was determined to make her feel like part of the family. Her mother-in-law-to-be had arrived twenty minutes ago by helicopter—she did like to make an entrance. Malee had introduced her to Yai, who thankfully wasn't wearing her tribal gear. Maybe some of Gran's crazy would rub off and help loosen up Caleb's mom.

All Malee's relatives were here as well, including her mother with her new husband. Bodin was strutting around as if he was responsible for the whole affair. Which, given the part he'd played in stranding her and Caleb together, wasn't too far from the truth. But no way was she letting him take credit for their love.

They were back where it all began. Destiny Resort had lived up to its name.

Since she'd agreed to move to Canada with Caleb, the hotel had undergone another transformation. It was now a stunning, if somewhat oversized, family home. They'd been back a few times to check on the renovations when they weren't busy scouting out new sites for Doyle Destinations. With Ian's blessing, the company was now going to concentrate on properties in Southeast Asia— Thailand, Vietnam, Laos, and Cambodia. Malee had taken on the official role of company translator. But it was the position as Caleb's lover she enjoyed the most.

"Hey there, handsome," she said, a slight catch in her voice as he turned at her words. His shirt perfectly matched his green eyes. But nothing could compare to the gleam of love in them.

"Malee." Her name slid off his lips as a breathless plea. The raw need in his voice struck a chord within her. "You are so incredibly beautiful."

Her aunt had made her a gorgeous raw silk dress in a luxurious cream color. It had a traditional Thai design with a gold-trimmed lace scarf draping across the front and over her shoulder to flow behind. The skirt flared out slightly below her knees and was edged with the same gold lace. Her mother had woven frangipani flowers through her hair, and she carried a bouquet of white roses and blue orchids tied with gold lace to match her dress.

"I came to make sure you weren't wearing a harness, ready to rappel down the side of the house." She ran a hand up his lapel and into the hair at his nape, tugging his head down for a kiss.

"Why didn't I think of that?" he whispered against her lips. She tried to deepen the embrace, but he held back. "I have to stand in front of a hundred people in a few minutes, babe. I'd rather not do it with a massive erection."

"As long as you promise me one later tonight."

"Tonight, and for the rest of our lives." This time he did kiss her, long and deep.

An elephant trumpet blast interrupted their embrace.

"Sounds like the guests are getting restless," she said with a laugh.

They'd hired a caretaker to look after the place when they weren't there, and to feed and try to control Steve, of course. The now-resident elephant wasn't pleased about all the extra people today, and Malee only hoped the arbor they'd set up to hold the ceremony hadn't been demolished.

"I'll go down now," Caleb said. He glanced at his trousers, where a discernible bulge distorted the front. "Start as you mean to go on, I guess." He shrugged and dropped another kiss on her cheek as he passed.

Malee took several deep breaths to cement this moment into her memories. Today was everything she'd ever dreamed of.

And it was just the beginning.

~~~~~~~

Thank you for reading *Thailand with the Tycoon*. Please post a review where you purchased the book. Your opinion will not only help other readers decide whether to buy the book or not, it will also help me continue to write the stories that I, and hopefully you, love to read. Thank you!

The Love in Translation series

continues with...

Bali with the Billionaire

He's all business. Until she makes him her business.

Harrison Mackenzie refuses to make the same mistake twice. Ever since tragedy shattered his life, he's locked his passion away to focus on work. Until a captivating woman without boundaries crashes through his meticulously constructed barriers to reach the billionaire's broken heart. Is he finally ready to risk loving again?

Jade Irvine is done with lying, cheating men. But that doesn't keep the Indonesian translator from the occasional no-strings-attached affair, especially with her handsome temporary employer. Surrounded by the beauty of Bali and fighting to open his spirit, she never expected that she'd fall so hard.

Struggling with intense emotions, Harrison and Jade try to keep things strictly physical until a shocking revelation forces the past and the present to collide.

Will a tropical fling change their lives forever?

Bali with the Billionaire

Chapter One

Jade Irvine smiled as she took in the refined elegance of the hotel lobby. It was definitely an upgrade from where she normally stayed when working in Bali. Except she wasn't working until tomorrow. Right now, she was on a hen weekend with her three best friends. And they'd be well on their way to partying if Jules wasn't having a "no, you hang up" Skype conversation with her boyfriend back in Australia.

"Oh, my God! Is that Henry Golding?" Lauren's high-pitched question had Jade, Karly, and a few other women scouting their surroundings. A giggle welled in Jade's throat. They probably looked like meercats to anyone who hadn't heard Lauren's question.

"Where?" Karly asked.

"Over there." Lauren nodded her head rather dramatically to the left.

The three friends peered into the hotel bar. A lone man sat apart from everyone else, his index finger circling the rim of the glass in front of him. Unfortunately, it wasn't a gorgeous actor needing a little cheer from four women celebrating an upcoming wedding. Still, he looked familiar…

"Actually, that guy's way hotter than Henry,"

Lauren—a self-professed expert on the male hotness scale—declared. "Is he a local? Jade, do you recognize him?"

She shook her head, still trying to place him. If they'd met in person, she'd never have forgotten him. She searched his features. "He looks sad," she said. "No one should be miserable in Bali. We should invite him to join us."

"Jade…" Karly and Laruen said in unison, warning tones in their voices.

"What?" she asked, flipping her long, dark hair over her shoulder, ready to go into action.

"We came to Bali to party before Karly voluntarily puts a noose around her neck," Lauren said. "Not so you can play Dr. Phil with a perfect stranger."

"It's a wedding ring, not a noose," Karly interrupted. The first of their tight-knit group to marry, she was ever ready to defend her decision to tie herself for life to one man.

Jade ignored the green-eyed monster whispering in her ear. If Keith hadn't been a lying bastard with a gangrenous heart, would she be as blindly hopeful heading toward the altar? Her eyes were automatically drawn back to the man at the bar. What was his story? Had his heart been shattered by a deceitful lover as well?

"I'm not playing Dr. Phil. But you have to admit he looks … lonely," Jade replied.

"He's not a koi fish that needs rescuing. Anyway, a guy that hot won't be lonely for long," Lauren said. As they watched, a scantily-clad woman approached him.

"What'd I miss?" Jules asked as she arrived, her face

all flushed. The Skype call must have gotten steamy before one of them came to their senses and hung up. "I thought we were going to Sky Garden. Are we having a starter drink here?"

They were the pick'n'mix of women. Karly, the bride-to-be, was blonde haired and blue eyed with the face of an angel and a laugh that made men hard. Jules had brown hair and eyes, and legs that went on forever. Lauren was the group's redheaded, hazel-eyed beauty with a legendary temper. But she was as fiercely loyal as a rescue dog. Wherever they went, they attracted male attention.

Karly exhaled a melodramatic sigh. "Jade wants to fix the guy at the bar."

"I don't want to *fix* him," Jade said, while Jules asked, "What guy?"

They all turned back to the magnificent specimen who was once again alone. The woman who had tried to talk to him earlier was now chatting on one of the sofas with a balding guy dressed in shorts and a flower-print shirt. It seemed someone was working tonight.

"See, he's alone again," Jade said, unable to take her eyes from the man. There was something about him that called to her.

He reached into the pocket of his suit jacket and pulled out a phone, giving the screen a long glance before he answered. Rotating in his seat, probably to hear better, he now faced them full-on. His eyes were distant, as though concentrating on the voice on the other end. But his countenance didn't light with joy as it would if he were speaking with a loved one.

"Do not get involved, Jade." Karly put her hands on her hips like some 1950s housewife scolding her child for tracking mud onto the freshly washed linoleum. Karly was always trying, mostly unsuccessfully, to mother the other girls.

"But—"

"Remember the cake," Lauren said.

"Come on, you cannot compare that man to a birthday cake," Jade protested.

"It was your idea that nearly burnt down the school," Lauren continued. "You just *had* to make a cake for the gardener, even though we weren't allowed in the kitchen and none of us had the slightest idea what we were doing."

"His mother had just died. No one else was going to give him a cake." And *she* wasn't the one who'd left the tea towel near the lit burner. Although it was her idea to cook the cake on the stovetop. With her culinary inexperience, she'd figured it had to be way faster than baking it in the oven.

"And the filing fiasco?" Jules added, unhelpfully.

Jade huffed. "I don't appreciate you bringing up all my minor mishaps."

"Mrs. Kiddy lost an entire year's lesson plans and the manuscript she'd been working on for five years. It was hardly a minor mishap." Karly raised her hand as Jade was about to interrupt. "I know your intentions were good. Yes, she was stressed and couldn't find anything on her messy desk, but sometimes, sweetie, you do more harm than good when you help." Karly put air quotes around the last word, eliciting a snort of laughter from

Jules.

"My favorite Jade misadventure was the bubble tsunami," Lauren added, like they were competing for the best disaster story.

The three other women dissolved into laughter. Karly wiped her cheeks as a few tears fell. "Only our Jade would have replaced the liquid laundry soap with bubble mix so the housekeeper's job wouldn't be so boring."

"There is no proof I did that," Jade said. Although she had. The poor woman had needed something to brighten her day. At least by then Jade had learned to cover her tracks in case things went sideways, as they inevitably did.

But this was different. The guy at the bar was a grown man. What harm could there be in inviting him for a drink and maybe a dance? "I still think we should ask him."

The four women peered into the bar again. The subject under discussion had completed his phone call and once more stared morosely into his drink.

"For once, I agree with Jade. I vote we bring him with us," Jules said.

For once, my arse. None of you girls need any convincing to follow me into trouble.

"You already have a boyfriend," Lauren reminded Jules.

"Yeah, but Sad-Man can watch our drinks while we get our groove on," Jules said. "Anyway, I was thinking maybe you could do with the company, Loly. It's been a while…"

Lauren made a face at Jules. "I'm focusing on my

career at the moment, thank you very much. Besides, what about Jade? She's unattached as well."

All three friends turned pitying eyes on her. "Jade's still in recovery," Karly said quietly, like they were discussing a potentially fatal diagnosis at the bedside of an unconscious relative.

Jade squared her shoulders. "I'm not in recovery. I'm over the scumbag. But for the record, I'm not looking for love, just a good time."

"A guy that hot… I'd put money on him being a good time," Lauren said with a nod toward the man at the bar.

Jade moved a little closer to the entryway to get a better view. "Crikey. Now I know why he looks familiar. I think that's my boss for the week."

"You're going to translate for *him*?" Karly asked. "Good luck with that. I doubt I'd even be able to speak English standing next to him."

Jade shrugged, feigning a bravado she definitely didn't feel. After years of faking it, though, few could tell the difference. "It's a tough job. But someone has to do it. Watch my back, ladies. I'm going in."

Her friends laughed as she strode into the bar to introduce herself. What were the chances she could manage it without saying something inappropriate?

***

Harrison Mackenzie sipped his scotch and glanced around the bar. This upscale Indonesian hotel had managed to combine the local architecture with western touches so a traveler felt both at home and on holiday.

Dark teakwood furniture was lightened with bright blue and red cushions. Tropical plants overflowed stone pots decorated with intricate Balinese carvings. Chrome lights and shiny glass surfaces gave a modern edge to the place. But not even the ever-swirling ceiling fans could dissipate the salty essence of the sea and the smell of coconut-scented sunscreen.

Too bad he wasn't on vacation. Although this was the last place he'd go to get away. Beaches and wild nightlife didn't appeal. He'd rather spend his off-work hours reading about ancient history. If he were to go abroad, it would be to an archaeological dig or someplace like Machu Picchu. He wouldn't hang out in a place known for the wild partying of its tourists. How the locals coped with the clash of cultures, he couldn't fathom.

"I could have gone in your place." Caleb's distant voice brought Harrison back to the phone conversation. "I know how tough Monday's date is for you." His friend must have forgotten that by crossing the date line, Harrison's Monday was tomorrow.

"It's fine. I'm fine. I … needed to get away this year."

Long pause. It could have been a problem with the connection from Canada, or maybe Caleb was figuring out what to say. "All right. But if you need me, I can be on the next plane out," Caleb said.

As if Harrison was going to ask his friend to hold his hand while Caleb's pregnant wife waited at home. He wasn't that selfish. Besides, marriage may have made his friend more open about his emotions, but that didn't mean Harrison was going to jump on that itchy hayride.

As long as he didn't let himself feel, everything would be okay.

Convincing Malee to marry him was the best negotiation Caleb had ever concluded. She was perfect for him, and his friend and business partner had never been happier. But sometimes Harrison longed for the time when the deepest thing Caleb said was, "Want another drink?" Not everyone got a happy ending to their story.

"I appreciate the support," Harrison answered. "Give my love to Malee."

"Will do."

Harrison toyed with the idea of turning off his phone to avoid more awkward calls, more people asking how he was doing. But considering his father's precarious health, he kept it on.

He barely had the device back in his pocket before another woman sauntered over to him. Her long ebony hair fell nearly to her waist. Well-rounded hips swayed in a provocative movement that struck a resonating tune within his body. The black dress she wore would give a thirteen-year-old boy wet dreams if he saw it on a hanger, never mind on this woman, with generous curves in all the right places. It didn't leave much to the imagination, except perhaps which sexual position to start with. She was everything he despised himself for wanting.

Without even a pause, she perched her gorgeous ass on the stool next to his, swinging a strappy-high-heel-clad foot so it almost brushed his calf. Up close, he could see that her eyes, which he'd expected to be dark like the rest of her coloring, were in fact deep green: pools of liquid emerald that lured him to forget the promises he'd made and drown in the desire she provoked. He shook his head to restart his brain, and her burgundy-stained lips parted in silent amusement.

"Are you waiting for your wife or girlfriend?" she asked without introducing herself. The middle finger of one hand was tightly pressed to her thumb, as though she'd been mid-meditation when she decided to proposition him.

"No, I have neither. I also don't pay for sex." Might as well move this encounter along so he could get back to nursing his whisky and going over his game plan for tomorrow's meetings. This was the first project to hit a snag since he'd become full partner in Caleb's investment firm. No way was he going to be bested by a painted design on a fricking T-shirt.

"Good to know. Have you ever had sex—free or otherwise?" The woman's Australian accent was a surprise. Until she'd opened her mouth, he'd pegged her for a local.

She flipped her hair over her shoulder, and Harrison's eyes were drawn to the long column of her neck. What sensuous delights would he experience as he tasted his way from her lips to her ear and then down her lightly tanned skin to her collarbone so prominently displayed? Not to mention her glorious breasts, pushed to the top of her dress as though waiting for an opportunity to escape the confines of the black silk fabric.

"Why do you ask that?" He could feel himself rising to her bait, a floundering sucker about to be enticed to his doom. *Never again.* Marshaling his inner iceman, he allowed his gaze to roam over her body before meeting her eyes with cool detachment—a look he'd perfected after years as a corporate lawyer. The expression told his competitors they were about to lose everything.

"You're so buttoned up. For God's sake, you're wearing a tie at a beach resort." She slid one black-polished fingernail down his blue-striped tie. He held his breath, praying the thing didn't catch fire. For a brief second, the urge to throw her over his shoulder and carry her upstairs to his suite flooded through him. But Harrison Mackenzie didn't lose control. Not anymore.

"I'm here on business."

She glanced around at the other patrons. Not one even wore a suit, never mind a tie. "I hate to break it to you, mate, but there's no one here to do business with."

"And you're not working?" He raised an eyebrow.

Her husky laugh enveloped him as she slid off her stool, putting her within inches of his body. He breathed in the scent of some exotic flower with a hint of ginger and lemongrass. Damn the hunger that gnawed at him.

"Nope. Not tonight, at least. I'm here to have fun. Besides, you can't put a price on this body."

He had to agree with her there.

"Enjoy your business," she said, and her husky voice was laced with humor. Before his brain could come up with a suitable response, she glided away, ignoring the ribald comments of a group of men drinking in the corner. He'd noticed them earlier, waving their money around and propositioning any woman who walked near. Harrison was perversely glad when the mystery woman kept walking. He'd hate to risk a tear in his suit jacket, rescuing her from their loutish behavior. Although given her confidence, she could probably defend herself.

At the door she glanced back at him once more, and he quickly turned away, annoyed that she'd caught him staring. Now he could get back to rehearsing his pitch for tomorrow. If it were a trial or contract negotiation, he'd be sure of his tactics. He knew exactly what he'd demand and where he could compromise.

This meeting, however, was different. He had to cajole and incentivize to get the project back on track. Find a way to get the other party to want to do more without offering anything in return. The venture was already bordering zero net, and they didn't have time to move to another manufacturer if they wanted to meet their pre-sales commitments. Plus, the whole discussion would be in Indonesian, and he'd have to rely on a translator to convey not only his words but his meaning, without revealing his desperation.

Giving up his legal career had been a no-brainer when he got to choose start-ups to fund and see through to IPO—it was exactly the kind of challenge he needed to forget everything he'd lost. Work was the one area of his life where he was now free to follow his passions. It would have to suffice.

He slung the rest of his whisky down his throat and made his way through to the lobby. His eyes searched for the woman in the black dress who'd talked to him in the bar, while his brain tried to reason that it would be better if he never saw her again. She was bold and brash and the exact opposite of everything his wife had been.

He shouldn't want to see her again—to run his fingers through her ink-black hair while he tasted her full lips. But he did. *Damn it.*

Get your copy of Bali with the Billionaire now!

Thank you, reader

I hope you enjoyed reading Caleb and Malee's story as much as I enjoyed writing it. If you did, **please, please** help others find it by leaving a **review** at your favorite retailer. Your review doesn't have to be long, but your opinion matters to me and other readers.

Want to be one of the first to know about upcoming releases, contests, and events? Sign up for my monthly newsletter at https://alexia-adams.com.

You can also chat with me on Facebook (https://www.facebook.com/AlexiaAdamsAuthor) and Twitter (@AlexiaAdamsAuth) or, of course, get in touch with me via my website (https://alexia-adams.com).

I love to hear from readers, so don't be shy.

About the Author

Alexia Adams was born in British Columbia, Canada, and traveled throughout North America as a child. After high school, she spent three months in Panama before moving to Dunedin, New Zealand, for a year, where she studied French and Russian at Otago University.

Back in Canada, she worked building fire engines until she'd saved enough for a round-the-world ticket. She traveled throughout Australasia before settling in London—the perfect place to indulge her love of history and travel. For four years, she lived and traveled throughout Europe before returning to her homeland. On the way back to Canada she stopped in Egypt, Jordan, Israel, India, Nepal, and of course, Australia and New Zealand. She lived again in Canada for one year before the lure of Europe and easy travel was too great, and she returned to the UK.

Marriage and the birth of two babies later, she moved back to Canada to raise her children with her British husband. Two more children were born in Canada, and her travel wings were well and truly clipped. Firmly rooted in the life of a stay-at-home mom, or trophy wife, as she prefers to be called, she turned to writing to exercise her mind, traveling vicariously through her romance novels.

Her stories reflect her love of travel and feature

locations as diverse as the windswept prairies of Canada to hot and humid cities in Asia. To discover other books written by Alexia or read her blog on inspirational destinations, visit her at https://Alexia-Adams.com or follow her on Twitter @AlexiaAdamsAuth

Other Books by Alexia:

Vintage Love series:

The Vintner and The Vixen

After witnessing a murder, Maya Tessier needs to disappear. So she escapes to the cottage in France she inherited from her great-grandmother where she hopes to start a new life and concentrate on her art. Jacques de Launay doesn't like strangers on his estate, especially when they're a sexy redhead who reminds him of all he's lost. But if he lets her stay, more than his heart may be at risk.

To read an excerpt, visit my website:

alexia-adams.com

The Playboy and The Single Mum

Single mother Lexy Camparelli must accompany super sexy Formula 1 driver Daniel Michaud for the rest of the race season as part of her job. Will she be able to keep her life on track and her heart from crashing or will the stress of living in the spotlight bring back her eating disorder or worse, jeopardize custody of her son?

To read an excerpt, visit my website:

alexia-adams.com

The Tycoon and The Teacher

Argentinian tycoon Santiago Alvarez will do whatever it takes to keep custody of his niece Miranda—even if it means marriage to the woman who jeopardizes his peace of mind. Genevieve Dubois is finding her way again after a traumatic experience left her unable to teach in a classroom. Helping an eight-year-old girl come to terms with the loss of her parents is challenge enough without the continual distracting presence of the sexy uncle who refuses to love. Then she discovers the real reason Santiago wants to retain guardianship of Miranda and it threatens all their futures.

To read an excerpt, visit my website:
alexia-adams.com

Guide to Love series:

Miss Guided

Mystery writer Marcus Sullivan is determined find someone for his younger brother Liam. Playing matchmaker on holiday in St. Lucia, Marcus tries to interest Liam in beautiful local tour guide Crescentia St. Ives. Then Marcus gets stranded with Crescentia and the plot to match her with his brother quickly incinerates in the flames of lust. No way can Liam have her when Marcus can't keep his hands off. Too bad he can't write a happier ending to their blossoming romance.

To read an excerpt, visit my website:
alexia-adams.com

Played by the Billionaire

Internet security billionaire, Liam Manning, made a promise to his beloved brother, Marcus, to complete his mystery-romance manuscript. Problem is that Liam's experience with women is limited to the cold-hearted supermodels he usually dates. So falling back on his hacking skills, he infiltrates an online dating site to find a suitable woman to teach him about romance—regular guy style. What he didn't expect was for the feelings to be so…real. Can Liam finish the novel before Lorelei discovers his deceptions and, more critically, before she breaches the firewall around his heart?

To read an excerpt, visit my website: alexia-adams.com

His Billion-Dollar Dilemma

Simon Lamont is an ice-cold corporate pirate. But when he arrives in San Francisco to acquire a floundering company and is accosted by a cute engineer with fire in her eyes, it takes all Simon has to maintain his legendary cool. Helen will do whatever it takes to change his mind, and if that means becoming the sexy woman Simon didn't know he wanted, so be it. If only she wasn't about to walk into her own trap...

To read an excerpt, visit my website: alexia-adams.com

Masquerading with the Billionaire

World-renowned jewelry designer Remington Wolfe is competing for the commission of a lifetime and someone is trying to destroy his company from the inside. He's in for more than one surprise when his unexpected rescuer turns out to be a sexy computer specialist with a sharp tongue and even sharper mind.

To read an excerpt, visit my website:
alexia-adams.com

Romance and Intrigue in the Greek Islands:

The Greek's Stowaway Bride

Hoping to make it to North Africa to free her uncle, Rania Ghalli stows away on the yacht of Greek millionaire Demetri Christodoulou. But when Egyptian agents board the boat, she can either jump overboard…or claim she's Demetri's new bride. Demetri needs a wife to complete a land purchase so he agrees to play along—if she'll agree to a real marriage. But keeping the vivacious woman out of his heart will be a lot harder than keeping her on his ship…

To read an excerpt, visit my website:
alexia-adams.com

Business Trip Romance:

Singapore Fling

Lalita Evans's father hired Jeremy Lakewood in the family's international conglomerate, and now he's tagging along as she oversees their interests across eight countries in three weeks. Will Jeremy risk his livelihood and all the success he's achieved to win the woman who haunts his dreams?

To read an excerpt, visit my website:
alexia-adams.com

An Inconvenient Series:

An Inconvenient Love

With the Italian economy in ruins, Luca Castellioni can't afford a distraction from running his successful property restoration company. However, he needs an English-speaking wife to cement a crucial deal. When his British bride-of-convenience undermines the foundations around his heart, he's forced to restructure his priorities. Is he too late for love?

To read an excerpt, visit my website:
alexia-adams.com

An Inconvenient Desire

Investment banker Jonathan Davis retreats to his Italian villa to lick his wounds post divorce, so his flirtation with runway model Olivia Chapman is just that. But when his ex dumps their toddler daughter on his doorstep, Olivia's assistance is a godsend that shakes up his world in more ways than one.

To read an excerpt, visit my website:
alexia-adams.com

Daring to Love Again Series:

The Sicilian's Forgotten Wife

Bella Vanni has accepted that her presumed-dead husband is long gone, so it's a huge shock when he knocks on her door and announces his desire to resume their marriage. She can't trust his answers on where he's been or why he left, and she certainly isn't keen to walk away from the life she's constructed for herself in his absence. But when Matteo's freedom is threatened, Bella must decide which is most important to her: everything she's painstakingly built or a second chance at a love that never died.

To read an excerpt, visit my website:
alexia-adams.com

Manufactured by Amazon.ca
Bolton, ON

29319453R00138